The Good Christian

The Good Christian

Dr. Steven Meyers and Quinn Haber

PhantaSea Books, Honolulu, HI
Back cover image by Kees Zwanenburg
Typeset by Amnet Systems

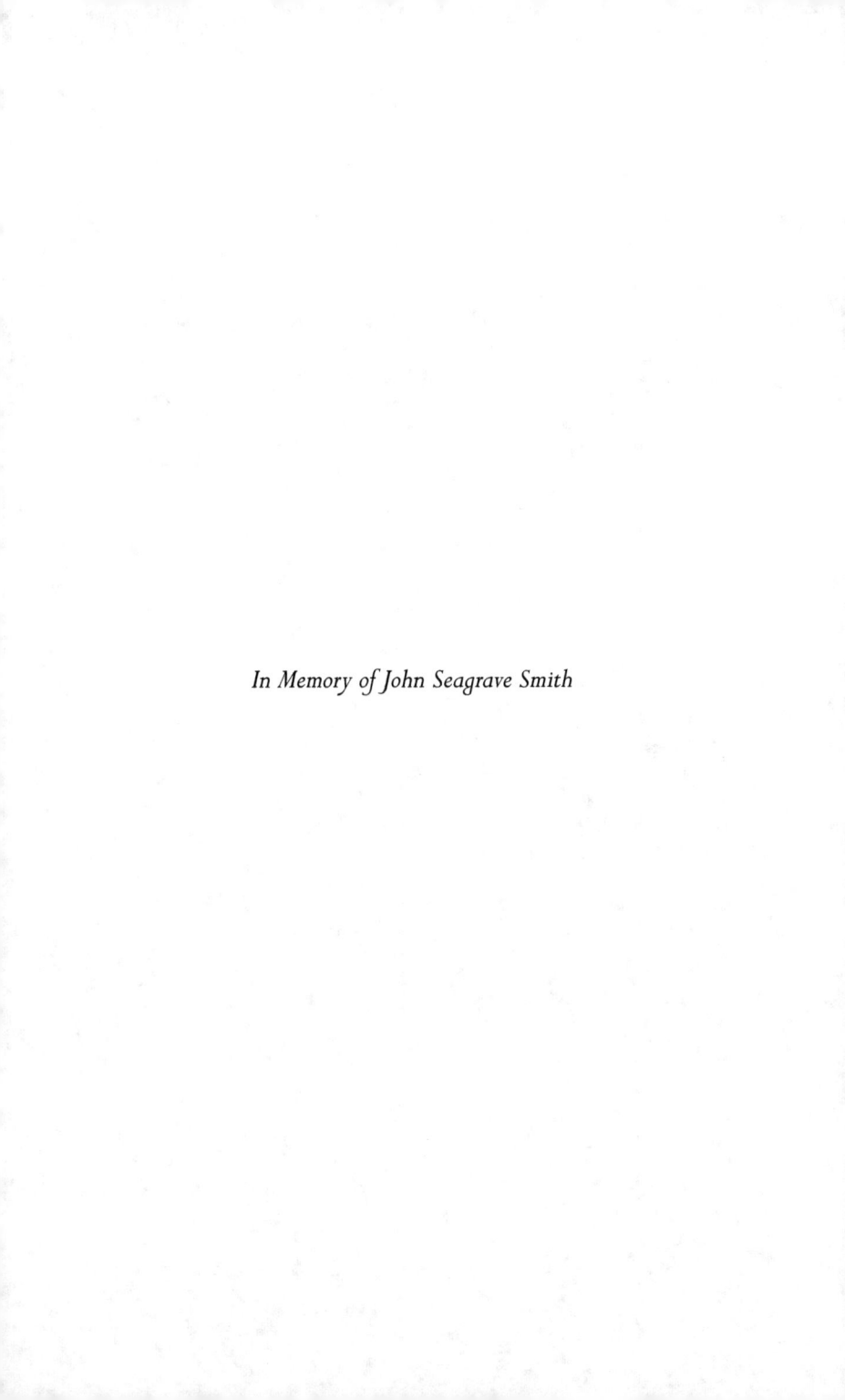

In Memory of John Seagrave Smith

Table of Contents

Acknowledgments

Special thanks to Edward Gregor, Paul Diamond, Sean Stratton, and Amnet Systems for their past assistance over various publishing platforms.

Thanks to Randy Lum, Miki Martins, Steven Long, and Michael Pinagiotis for standing apart from the silent majority.

Thanks to Ari Marsh, and Eric Holland, for living and sharing their wealth of spiritual knowledge.

Thanks to Richard Dusendschon for his tireless advocacy for persons with disabilities.

Thanks to Brian Pisanelli for his chivalry in the blue.

And most of all, thanks to our families, who tolerate the time we require to write.

For Christ's sake!

I delight in weaknesses, in insults,

In hardships, in persecutions, in difficulties.

For when I am weak, I am strong.

—— *Corinthians 12:10*

Prologue

August 12, 2013

Chris Fields walked the several blocks between his service sector job and his retail job. He wore black "shiner" faux leather shoes, khaki trousers, and a light blue collared shirt. A timeworn English briefcase, its strap slung over his shoulder, dangled by his side. He was making haste, because his next shift started at 4:30 p.m. and it was already 4:25 p.m. Rush hour was well underway in Honolulu, with people buzzing about the byways and queuing up at the bus stops.

As he pattered along the sidewalk, the first clues to his uncommon behavior were making themselves manifest to anyone who happened to be watching, and today that casual observer was me.

A group of several heavyset individuals were heading toward him, taking up the entire breadth of walkway as they advanced. Moseying shoulder-to-shoulder as they chatted, they weren't paying much attention to where they were going other than down the sidewalk. When Chris drew upon their position, he turned himself sideways with his handbag in an attempt to pass to one side. Several of them took notice, but made no effort at allowing him passage, the end result being his detouring into an adjacent municipal planter box, where he took a further step back into the foliage and offered them a brief bow of recognition. They paid no mind to his antics, as they continued plodding by, and so he continued on around them through the lowly plants.

Introduction

My name is Dr. Steven Meyers. I'm originally from Michigan, but currently live in Honolulu, where I work for the Hawaii State Department of Health as a clinical psychologist for troubled adults, many of whom are street people, or homeless. I have decided to maintain a private journal, beginning with the entry mentioned earlier, concerning a certain Chris Fields—a young man of twenty-four who was recently added to my caseload via a care coordinator who reported he required the attention of a mental health specialist beyond the level of social worker. Social workers are trained to treat a relatively mild set of standardized aberrant behaviors, but when they encounter subjects such as Chris Fields who are deemed to carry "elevated complex behaviors," such cases are often forwarded to professional psychologists for further evaluation. Chris acquired an organizational record with Hawaii state mental health programs due to prior referrals from his probation officer (PO), but only recently, as his case fell under stricter review guidelines, was his docket upgraded beyond social worker involvement.

My investigation thus far into Chris's clinical record presents a persona so singularly baffling that this journal shall serve as a personal workshop of sorts, where I can input my own raw data about him before I draw formal conclusions for his psychological record, which I am required to file with the state. Such a record might remain accessible to authorized health and legal entities for the rest of the patient's life, and so it is of utmost importance, as a clinical psychologist, that I assign a correct diagnosis to my subject from the start.

The overarching theme to Chris's abstract is akin to that of a miscast play actor: he is frequently in trouble with the law and always concedes blame to himself, yet those on record who know him publicly and the few who know something of his private side describe a character so benevolent that I am inclined to believe him more saint than recidivist.

As I begin my own investigation into the formative events that have led to Chris's singular personality, objective, formal psychology presents a wide array of possible causes that must be taken into full consideration, even if they run in contrary to my own empirical observations. The human mind is like an onion: the way people behave on the surface reveals only their outer, social layer—their personality. But what lies beneath is often shy and elusive. My duty is to penetrate all the way through to the core, where the mind holds close concert with the heart and soul, for only there can the healing of the entire individual begin, and only then can the music of their life be made sweet again as is their God-given birthright.

The log to follow (continuing from the prologue) will post my actual observations and clinical encounters with Chris as near as possible to the time of their occurrences—usually I am able to complete my entries on the same day. Only at the conclusion will I offer any decisive analysis.

Dr. Steven Meyers, PsyD

Observations and Encounters

August 12, 2013, continued . . .
Nearing Chris's secondary place of employment, Hometech Hut, I cut off into a diner across the street called Zippy's as he continued into work. I'd been shadowing him during his several blocks' transfer between workplaces, taking the opportunity to observe him in his natural environment before formal contact was made. There was a big sale going on in his store, and I was in the market for a new laptop, anyway, so it was a golden opportunity to study him in action prior to our actual meeting. Once I start a relationship with a client (a.k.a. patient) in a clinical sense, it invariably affects their behavior while I am in their presence by heightening their self-awareness. My primary objective now was to see Chris acting in his normal manner as I sought out a new computer.

Shortly after 5:00 p.m., I entered the store and proceeded to the computer display tables, where a sales associate briefed me on the current promotion. I did not see Chris at first, but soon noticed him talking to a customer near the flat screen TVs. As I continued browsing the laptops, I watched him assisting customers left and right, dashing to and fro to fulfill their needs, the floor manager all the while giving him new directives to complete.

After a while, when Chris drew near me, I called out to him: "Excuse me sir, I have a question."

He rushed over and replied in a chipper tone, "Yes sir, how may I help you?"

I sought direct eye contact with him, but his focus was somehow crooked, with one eye looking in a slightly different direction than the other. Beyond that, he looked tired, with dark rings encircling his off-kilter stare, while his forehead was creased with too many wrinkles for his age.

"Do the salespeople make commission on these?" I inquired, pointing to the computers.

"We do, actually."

"Okay, great! I'll take this one and you can make the sale."

"The HP?" he replied. "Sure. Do you have any questions about it?"

"The promo comes with free MS Office Suite and the antivirus package, is that right?"

"Yes, sir, we can get everything configured for you. Let me check in the——"

"Chris!" the floor manager trumpeted from behind us. "I need you on phones at the front counter, now!"

"This is Scott, sir," Chris introduced the interlocutor. "He will take care of you."

I turned to Scott and said, "I want to make sure that Chris here gets the commission on this HP Pavilion I'm about to buy."

"Don't worry about that, sir," Chris interjected, and then made haste to the front counter, where the lines were lengthening by the minute.

Scott went into the back to retrieve the new stock of my chosen laptop and some software, and then met me at the far side of the checkout counter, where he began unboxing the items. As for Chris, at first he was helping ring up sales several registers down, but then came beside us to configure a new smartphone. The customer he was serving, a Caucasian near his own age, wore a backwards baseball cap over long blonde locks and sported thick gold chains, while a big fellow standing in close company behind him had bulldoggish features, a tattooed neck, and wore a long-sleeve flannel shirt with only the top button fastened, beneath which his khaki, Bermuda shorts extended down to his shins, over which white, high drawn socks ran the rest of the way down to his black "wino" shoes. In short, the duo emulated a style of gangbangers, if they really were or not.

"So you wanted the prepaid Nokia?" Chris reconfirmed with the blonde one in front.

"That's right, prepaid," the customer replied; and then his henchman behind handed him a separate phone and said, "It's for you, boss."

As Chris set about programming the Nokia, the blonde guy began transacting a drug deal over the phone his henchman had handed him, talking about "fronting," "ounces," and "da kine," this latter being a Hawaiian pidgin (slang) way of referring to something without actually saying what it is. When he was done with the call, he looked up and said, "So hey, Chris, how's the HomeTech gig paying off?"

"Excuse me?" Chris inquired.

"Dumb ass," grumbled the larger one behind, eliciting a chuckle from himself and his blonde crony in front.

"You know," continued the blondie, "where's the fucking beef, Chris? Why waste your time with a job like this?"

"It's a good job," Chris replied, then handed him the newly configured handset and said, "Here's your new Nokia. The number is on the removable sticker inside, with instruction on how to change the password. I hope it serves you well."

"Serves me well," huffed the cantankerous customer in soliloquy. "What the fuck do you know? Have a fuck-all day, Chris."

The thugs turned to leave, when Chris held out a small, squared bag and said, "The box and receipt, sir."

"Fucking clown," the crony behind uttered as they continued out the door.

"I'm sorry I couldn't serve you better," Chris called out in vain as the door closed behind them.

The next customer in line, a middle-aged woman clutching a phone in its box, stepped forward with a glum expression and said, "I want to buy this Samsung Reclaim."

"Sure thing, ma'am, I can help you with that," Chris answered, holding out a hand.

While Scott continued to configure my new laptop, I watched as Chris tried to activate the woman's new smartphone, but he fumbled on one of the last steps and soon found himself on the store's landline trying to get in touch with the customer service department of the national carrier to rectify the problem.

About ten minutes later, Chris was still on hold and his customer was growing restive. He explained to her that the national carrier was located on the mainland and their call center was receiving a high volume of calls at that hour, and probably with reduced staff moreover. The woman had already paid for the Reclaim, which was an ecologically friendly handset fashioned from recycled materials and ultimately biodegradable. But her patience had already expired. She slammed her palm against the counter and shook a finger before Chris's nose, demanding to speak to the manager.

"Please, ma'am, just a few more minutes?" Chris entreated. "I'm just getting through to the carrier."

"I don't have time for this shit!" the woman ranted. "You're useless! I want to speak to the store manager, now!"

"I'm sorry, ma'am, but he's on break offsite," Chris replied.

She turned to Scott with quivering lips and exhorted, "You can help me, right?"

Scott pointed lazily back at Chris and said, "Sorry, ma'am, but he's gotta do it. It's the way postpaid accounts are set up in our system."

"Well then, I want my money back!" she fumed. "I'm out of time!"

"Can you come back in thirty minutes?" Chris implored. "I should have the phone ready by then."

"Where's the manager? Give me my money back!" She was relentless.

Chris procured his wallet.

"Oi, Chris!" Scott warned. "You know you can't transfer that phone to your name or anyone else's." He then continued to the irate woman: "It's the way a customer's name and billing address are set up on a postpaid account. Once the phone is paid for, it's linked to that person and we can't change it from here due to Federal laws designed to track terrorists."

"But it's not even activated yet!" she reproached.

"It doesn't matter, ma'am—the phone has already been paid for and your information is already entered into our system, however wrongly." He shot a wry glance at Chris.

"Your personal PIN has already been entered," Chris explained, "and that's a big part of the problem."

The termagant's expression grew bitterly cross and she began to visibly shake, at which point Chris hung up the landline and handed her the Reclaim along with a wad of cash, saying, "Here's the phone along with a full refund. I'm terribly sorry I was unable to activate it, but if you want to leave it with me, I can finish the setup tonight and you can come back anytime tomorrow to pick it up."

"*Hmpfh!*" she puffed, stuffing the money and handset into her purse. She tromped toward the exit, but stopped just short of the door to deliver the Reclaim back to Scott, instructing loudly, "Tell that idiot over there I'll be back tomorrow to reclaim this, and by god, it better be activated!"

Scott transferred the handset back to Chris, who had just finishing counting the three dollars remaining in his wallet.

Not long after the shrew had left, the manager returned and got wind of what had happened. "Why do you keep doing that?!" he scolded Chris under his breath as he proceeded to help the cashiers behind the counter, for the lines had grown even longer in his absence and the customers were frowning and agitated.

"I'm sorry," Chris replied, "but she didn't want to wait. She was really mad and so I returned her money. But I can finish the activation and she will pick up the handset tomorrow."

"You're not supposed to keep issuing refunds from your own pocket," he admonished, "and you know that. It's not in store policy. You keep fumbling the phone setups. Just finish the activation and then clock out. I'll talk to you about this on your next shift."

"I'm sorry, boss," Chris diffidently conceded, and then he bagged another customer's purchase and handed it to them, saying, "Thank, you, come again."

"The activation!" the manager scolded. "Do it now!"

Chris turned and once again picked up the landline, but this time he got through to the telecom carrier right away and was able to rectify the botched setup in just a few minutes. He left the newly activated phone on the rear counter with a note, and then disappeared into the staff room in the back, emerging moments later with his briefcase slung over his shoulder. He made a hasty retreat out the front door while never looking up from the floor.

—⚏—

Scott carefully replaced my new laptop back into its box and said, "You're all set, the configuration is complete." He transferred it next to the cashier adjacent, along with a set of barcodes relating the software promo.

As the clerk was entering my purchase, she stepped aside to allow Scott to input some information of his own.

"Thanks for helping with the setup," I told him, "but I want Chris to get the commission. He made the sale."

Scott paused and looked to the manager, who had been keeping a glancing eye on the transaction.

"I'm sorry, sir," the manager informed me, "but that won't be possible. Chris has already punched out for the day."

I shook my head and had a mind to cancel the sale, but with the store transaction and credit card capture slips already printing up, I capitulated to the settlement.

"You know," I told the manager as I begrudgingly signed the receipts, "that was a really noble thing for Chris to do, paying for the woman's phone like that."

"Maybe so," he said, "but it's not in store policy and sets a bad precedent. The Samsung Reclaim is on closeout promo and as such is nonrefundable, but beyond that, ever since the Boston Marathon bombings, postpaid cell phone registrations have been put under strict Federal guidelines. They're trying to track the bad guys, you know. But that's where Chris screwed up. I'm very sorry about that, sir—he's had ample training. But he'll soon figure out that he can't afford it. Next customer!"

August 13, 2013

Today I met with Chris's care coordinator, Karen B., over lunch to discuss Chris's prior IEP and his recent clinical evaluations. (An IEP, or Individualized Education Program, is a document pertaining to an individual's needs for special education up to age twenty-one.) We chose the most isolated table in the restaurant on South King Street, because by law, all clinical matters pertaining to patients enrolled in state disability programs are strictly confidential. As we reviewed some of the documents over steaming pots of *Pho*, it became clear to me that Chris didn't have a disability so much as he had exhibited several delays. His K-12 educational summary, and a report pertaining to his two years in junior college, indicated a significant delay in math, a disinterest in curricular sports and social functions, and a lack of academic direction. He averaged two courses per semester in junior college—all electives—and had not yet chosen a particular degree. But he excelled in music and did well in the humanities, and registered an impeccable attendance record in all his classes. His last referring social worker suggested he be evaluated for an autism spectral disorder.

"What about his police record?" I asked Karen. "You mentioned he had a rap sheet?"

She handed me two documents from the Honolulu Police Department. The first, dated January 31 of this year, was a misdemeanor charge for petty theft from a convenience store, and the second was a citation from two years ago, when he got busted for drinking beer on a beach in Waikiki.

"What else? Any felonies?"

"I seem to have left the other police reports in my office," she replied. "He's been incarcerated several times since high school on misdemeanor charges, but no, no felonies that I know of. City jail stints only, nothing Federal. There are two more charges of petty theft from stores here in Hawaii, and another one for indecent exposure, from what I recall."

"Indecent exposure?"

"He was cited for swimming in the nude at San Souci Beach early one morning."

"Off Diamond Head?"

"Yes, that's the place. Seems harmless enough, but unfortunately for Chris, that beach is very family friendly."

"I wonder just how early he was doing that. Five o'clock in the morning versus eight would tell me a lot about his social awareness."

"I believe it was 6:30 a.m., but I can check."

"Yes, please do. What about his parents? I understand they live back East and are not particularly involved in his life at this point?"

"Chris left home shortly after graduating from high school. Apparently, his parents didn't want him around the house if he wasn't going to work that summer, and since he had trouble finding a job right away, he went to Los Angeles to stay with his uncle. But that only lasted several weeks before his father mailed him a final check to enable him to move to Hawaii, where he was keen on finding a job and enrolling in junior college."

"Which he did."

"Yes, eventually."

"What was the trouble with his parents growing up?"

"Chris is the youngest of three siblings, and his parents seemed to have nitpicked on him a lot more than the others, which he construes as being unwanted. That's about all we could get from him about his family life. He's shy to public scrutiny, while in a therapeutic setting, when pressed, he always concedes blame for his problems and missteps, citing his own perceived shortcomings while glossing over other possible causative factors."

"There is a bit of pattern then, isn't there?"

"What complicates things is, he has an obsession with behaving properly, yet he commits these acts of petty theft. His social life seems to be direly lacking, so he may be lashing out."

"Seeking attention?"

"Perhaps," Karen deemed. "But he's refused to see us after his last probation expired, you know—elusive as ever. How do you intend to encounter him?"

"I think I know how I can help him. He has no social life because he works two full-time jobs and is taking classes. I may try to afford him a few days a week of reprieve from his jobs for undisclosed, state sanctioned 'medical reasons.' There are financial needs tools that I might able to leverage, such as tuition and disability benefits, if I can effect a formal declaration by way a particular ICD-9 clinical diagnosis—a professional evaluation that could legally entitle him to things like a reduction in stress and more rest to aid in his treatment."

"Like with CFS," Karen posited.

"Yes, precisely—although chronic fatigue syndrome is obviously not his problem, there are other diagnoses that carry similar benefits that I can explore as I gain collateral information about his behaviors. Mind you, I am in no way suggesting gaming the system or anything like that. Rather, I will study the most appropriate range of possible diagnoses and then explore what sort of financial tools might be available from there, to help offset his reduction in pay while I work with him. Short-term measures, you know, until I can help him get on better footing, psychologically speaking."

"Do you think he needs meds?"

"Probably not, but I won't know for certain until I start face-to-face intervention."

"Well, I'm glad you have a plan, Steven," she confided over a sip of hot, green tea. "He's so young still, has whole life ahead of him, but you know how it goes when they refuse to meet outside of parole. I hate seeing people pinball around in their own recurring behaviors, in and out of recidivism, when we can help them in the interim."

"Yes, I know. Don't worry, Karen—I'll get his ball moving in my direction ASAP."

"Thank you, doctor."

"It is my duty." I told the ever-industrious care coordinator, then requested the check from the waiter and paid for the two of us, with Karen leaving the tip. Not exactly going Dutch, but my salary superseded hers by a long shot.

August 15, 2013

Yesterday I submitted to Sue Tamura, the executive director of the Hawaii Department of Health division that employs me, an individualized funding request for Chris's case. Today, while I was awaiting her response, presumably in the form of an approval, Chris was referred directly back to our program by his PO on account of a new report submitted by the Honolulu Police Department. Chris had not committed another crime, but was an "active witness" to one, the HPD report stated, and his behavior in the matter "requires the prompt attention of the Honolulu adult mental health authorities."

Before I paraphrase what had actually transpired, it should be noted that the incident, however troubling, proved serendipitous in its timing, because now Chris, shy to public scrutiny, by law had to return to our offices for further therapy, and his rehabilitation was now squarely in my aegis.

In the police report, filed several days ago, Chris was cited with "obstructing security officers in the interference of their personal duties" at AmeriMart superstore on Ke'eaumoku Street. While Chris was waiting in line at one of the checkout counters, store security descended upon the customer in front of him. This customer, hereafter "the suspect," put up fierce resistance, whereupon several high-capacity USB flash drives were forcibly ejected from his pockets—store merchandise the security officers aver the suspect was attempting to shoplift from the electronics department.

In observing the fracas before him, Chris came to the suspect's defense, claiming that he had planted the flash sticks on the suspect without the suspect's knowing it. Chris was apprehended along with the suspect and conveyed to the store security office, where the police arrived shortly thereafter.

In reviewing the CCTV footage, the police observed the suspect in the electronics section using a razorblade to re-move three USB "thumb drives" from their packages before stashing them in his windbreaker's right-hand pocket. Chris, meanwhile, was in the produce section selecting a banana, and afterward, he went to the beverages section to obtain a bottle of water—both areas being nowhere near the elec-tronics section, and completely out of sight of, in fact. In reversing the video back further, the police observed the suspect arriving inside the store approximately four minutes before Chris, and at no time did they make contact with one another while in the store until the fracas at the checkout counter.

When the suspect was initially asked by the store security officers if Chris had placed the flash sticks in his pocket, he replied, "He must have, because I didn't do it."

It was only during the CCTV review in the presence of the police that the suspect postulated he may have pocketed the flash sticks "by accident," and that he did not know Chris prior to the incident, at which point Chris came to his defense again, stating emphatically, "But I *made him* take the flash sticks, *I* am responsible, and you ought to let him go."

When asked how he "made" the suspect take the flash sticks, Chris replied, "I coerced him before we entered the store."

"How did you coerce him?" the police asked.

"I just told him that I was going to make him do it," he replied.

"You threatened him?"

"Yeah, I did," Chris maintained.

The suspect nodded in agreement of Chris's statement, so was pressed further about his prior knowledge of Chris. He fumbled with a new storyline before admitting again that he had never met Chris prior to the fracas at the checkout counter. The police subsequently scrolled through the suspect's cell phone contacts list and did not find Chris's name or number. The suspect was handcuffed and taken away on shoplifting charges, while Chris was cited and released.

Chris's citation for obstructing a security officer landed on the desk of his PO, who forwarded it to us along with a state-sanctioned order for his psychiatric evaluation. Chris was lucky: if he had tried to obstruct a police officer and not a security officer, he may have been charged with a misdemeanor offence including a jail sentence of up to one year and fine of up to US$1000. A worst case scenario could have seen him facing an obstruction of justice ruling, which can carry far steeped penalties, including a felony judgment. But obviously, he was mentally disturbed.

In receiving the PO's certified letter for mandatory inpatient rehabilitation at our program offices, Sue Tamura consequently signed off on my patient respite therapy-funding request for Chris's case, providing two-months' financial assistance for him to take two days off per week from his jobs if he abided by the respite order while undergoing psychiatric evaluation and therapy under my care.

The last action I took today on this case was in emailing the PO to coordinate Chris's first appointment with me. My next entry will report directly on that intake session.

August 20, 2013

My intake encounter with Chris transpired today, four days after I had emailed his PO. This was the soonest Chris could come in on account of his busy work and school schedule, according to the PO.

Meeting Chris at the reception counter, I introduced myself and we shook hands. He made brief eye contact with me, and then squinted in a downward direction as if in intense concentration. He was sweating at the brow, perhaps on account of his just coming in from Hawaii's August humidity, and appeared substantially enervated. As we walked toward my office, he kept his focus on the floor.

We stopped before the office kitchenette, where I offered him water from the dispenser.

He took the plastic cup with a polite "Thank you," and then regarded me with slightly crossed eyes and asked, "Don't I recognize you from someplace?"

"I was in Hometech Hut not long ago," I replied, as I reached for a porcelain mug in the cabinets. "You helped with a computer, remember?"

"Oh yeah, that's it."

"There were a few bossy customers there," I added with a sympathetic twinkle, "and your bossy boss."

He cast his eyes down again, answering naught.

After fixing myself a cup of hot tea, I conveyed him into my office.

—⚎—

Chris placed his cup on the table between us, and then sat down and folded his arms over his English briefcase.

"So do you ever go by Christopher, or Christian?" I prompted as I stirred my tea, easing into things. "Or is Chris the sum of your first name?"

"It's just Chris, sir."

"Steven, Chris—you can call me Steven. I know how busy you must be between work and college, so I appreciate your making the time to come in today."

Of course, he was now legally bound to meet with me, but it was important to extend an olive branch over the baton of judicial imperative.

"When I was your age," I offered, "I was doing the same thing—working my way through school. I have a lot of respect for what you're doing, Chris, because I know it isn't easy."

He stared down at the edge of the table, not answering.

I tapped my teaspoon against my cup's rim, sounding off three bright tinkles, and then continued, "So how's it going with all that?"

"It's okay, I guess." He leaned forward and took his first sip of the water.

"Not bad, but not that great, I take it?"

He scanned the doctorate's certificates on the wall behind my desk. "So it looks like you're a pretty big time practitioner," he offered.

I chuckled self-effacingly and leaned back in my chair. "Not that big time, Chris. If I were, I probably wouldn't be practicing with the state."

"Why do you say that?"

"Because government employment is public-services oriented, while most doctors with my qualifications tend toward private practice, which is far more lucrative."

"So why do you do it, then?"

"Public service? Because I wanted to live in Hawaii, and the state of Hawaii needed clinical psychologists, and so I applied and was accepted, and have been here ever since. I enjoy serving the people of Hawaii, and I'll tell you something, Chris, I'm not missing winters in Michigan one bit. I understand you're from Los Angeles originally?"

"No, I'm from South Carolina, but I went to Los Angeles briefly before I moved out here to work and go to college."

"I was going to ask you about that, but first," I paused, not wishing to try his intelligence by tiptoeing any further around the elephant in the room, "we should talk a little bit about why you were referred here by you PO: the incident at AmeriMart. You took the blame for another's crime. That's noble of you, but it's going to get you into heaps of trouble, if it hasn't already. Something tells me that your prior offences for petty theft perhaps shouldn't belong to you either, does that sound about right?"

He looked down.

"Chris?"

"One must take it upon themselves to be responsible," he mumbled, but the response was manifest.

"But not for *other's* crimes, Chris. Look, we all feel guilty about something, something big or something small, but the way to fix it to deal with the cause of it, and not keep piling blame upon ourselves for things we really are not responsible for."

He scrunched and lowered his brows, his eyes darting furtive glances over the tabletop, but never at me.

"Chris, I think we should start from the beginning. I have about twenty questions that I usually ask of new referrals. It's a way for me to get better acquainted with them, to try to see the bigger picture of their lives and what might be bothering them. They're like standard intake questions, but more informal—just between us, you know what I mean?"

He exhaled a heavy breath and then slightly gnawed on his lower lip, his eyes slanting up at mine. "Okay then, Doctor Meyers, what are your questions?"

I stirred my tea again, sounding off some deeply sunken rings before setting the mug aside. "Well, for starters, where do you live?"

He appeared perplexed by the question. "I don't know—I guess I'm just doing what I can."

"But where do you live, Chris, in an apartment?"

"Oh, *where* do I live. I thought you asked, '*why* do I live.' Yes, I share an apartment with five other people in Waimanalo."

"How do you commute to town every day?"

"I catch one of the early buses in, and ride the last one out."

"Long day, huh?"

"I work two jobs and have classes twice a week at Kapiolani Community College."

"Do you like your living situation now?"

"I live in a section of the living room that's been cordoned off into three smaller rooms by sheets of plywood, forming my own little space. It's pretty much a matchbox, but I only pay $400 a month, and I get the lanai, which is pretty cool. I keep my upright piano stored there under a tarp, because there's not enough room inside."

"Do you play it often?"

"I rarely have the time anymore."

"And your roommates—are they working students, too?"

"One of them is an older Hawaiian guy; he's like retired or on welfare or something. He just likes to fish a lot. He's cool, but we rarely see each other, which is probably a good thing, because he smokes a lot of cigarettes and the smoke bothers me. I'm rarely home except to sleep. The other person sharing the partitioned living room with me is a Filipina lady about forty-five years old who works as a housekeeper at one of the Waikiki hotels. There's also a Filipino student who has his own room—he's about my age. I don't think he's home much either, but I sometimes catch him up late at night, playing video games on his computer and smoking marijuana. Then there are these two guys that split the far bedroom, also with partitions. One is an older, Korean security guard. I once saw black leather masks and whips and stuff around in his hovel, so I try to stay away from him. His roommate is this *haole* guy about ten years older than me who looks really screwed up mentally—I think his dad was a major alcoholic or something. Anyway, I think he used work in an office, but quit and is now trying to be a writer or something. He's there all the time, from what I can gather. Sometimes, when he's up early cooking breakfast, I see him smashing his eggs in the pan with a spatula, like really angrily, cursing at them while beating them. He always leaves a big mess, too. Once I slipped on a chunk of boiled broccoli he left on the floor and hit my head pretty hard against the linoleum. Sometimes he forgets to turn off the fryer, and if it wasn't for me a few times, I think he would have started a major fire. It gets me worried, but what can I do? The others don't do anything about it, and I'm too busy to babysit him. Aside from my piano, my personal belongings are minimal, so I just let it go."

"Sounds quite tenuous. So you all pretty much stick to yourselves, then?"

"Yeah, but it could be worse, I guess. The apartment only has one bathroom, but I usually get it first in the morning because I'm up super early."

"So your living situation is cramped, maybe even a little dangerous, but it's affordable, and that's why you're there—is that an accurate assessment?"

"Truth be told, I can barely afford it. I have a lot of debts to pay on top of rent. But it is what it is, and this is where I'm at."

"Okay, Chris, maybe this is one area we can try to improve upon—your current living situation."

He shook his head. "I don't really care—rent is cheap and I'm rarely there; it's just a place to hang my head."

"Well, do be careful, Chris. Turn on the kitchen lights in the morning, and watch your step. Okay, let's move on, then: Can you tell me what it was like growing up with your family?"

He frowned at my question, at last answering: "I was in trouble a lot."

"With your parents?"

"With them, at school . . . I was the black sheep of the family, although I never wanted to be. My behavior was not good. I think I cried a lot as a baby, and just failed my parents' expectations."

"Why would you say you cried a lot as a baby? You're not supposed to be expected to control your emotions at such an early age, but you think your parents were displeased by it?"

"That's the only way I can figure out how I bothered them so much early on. I was just a troublemaker, you see, and it all seems to have started when I was very young."

"I see. I understand you have siblings? Can you tell me something about them?"

"Yeah, I have an older brother and sister. My brother is eight years my senior, and always just wanted me out of his hair. My sister, Rachel, was my parents' favorite. She got straight A's in school, and they were always supportive of her activities like glee club and prom night and stuff."

"Were your parents supportive of any of your activities or interests?'

"Maybe at first. My mom started me off on piano lessons when I was eleven, and my dad put me into Boy Scouts, but I started getting into trouble left and right, and when I stopped going to Boy Scouts, I think my dad just had enough of me."

"What kind of trouble were you getting into?"

"In Boy Scouts?"

"In general."

"Things like throwing rocks, getting bad grades, sometimes breaking stuff in the house, and I got arrested once in Newport Beach for smoking pot. I thought my dad was going to kill me. I knew he was super angry, but he just kept a steely-eyed expression and gave me a short speech about how I went wrong. And that's the way he still looks at me today, just totally disappointed and pissed off. Whenever I see him now, he just shakes his head and smacks his lips, 'tsk-tsk-tsk.'"

"How old were you when that incident happened in Newport Beach?"

"About fourteen. That was the first time I ever got arrested."

"Has you father ever hit you or anything like that?"

"Sometimes he used to hit me with his comb. It didn't hurt much, but left an impression like a little shotgun with all these little prick-marks. He once chased me around the house with a hammer, when my brother broke the Jacuzzi and blamed it on me. I was really terrified of my dad and just wanted to get away from him."

"Can you remember some other incidents when he really scared you?"

"Yeah, when I failed government in high school, I had to go with him to talk to the principal about that and other things I was screwing up in. When we got home, he just went ballistic and chased me around from room to room, admonishing me severely and calling me a shame to him and the family. Another time, I was fighting with my sister and pushed her over. She fell back and broke her wrist on the floor and had to go to the hospital. My dad really laid into me then, slapping me around real hard with his comb, and then he grounded me for like a month. He just didn't like me—I was a real piece of shit in his eyes, and in retrospect, he probably was right, and I deserved it, mostly."

"I see how you must feel, given the circumstances, but let's not rush to judgments so soon. You mentioned you sometimes broke things at home. What kind of things? Did you do it on purpose?"

"Once my sister accidentally tipped over my parents' favorite statue and broke it, then she blamed it on me. That was really bad."

"And you took the blame?"

"I told them what happened, but they believed her instead. They always believed her, so it doesn't matter—I broke a lot of stuff, too. Once I really couldn't stand myself and so I socked my reflection in the bathroom mirror. I told my dad it was an accident, and he made me pay for it through my allowance. And then there was this time I fell asleep with a candle burning on top of a plastic Halloween skull I had. The fire alarm went off at three o'clock in the morning. My room was filled with smoke and the table was on fire. I quickly put it out before my parents came in and pretended I was still asleep, because I wanted to look innocent. But they were more worried than mad. I think they were just thankful I was still alive, or that the house didn't burn down. I thought that after that, they would probably pay closer attention to me and everything I did, but it was sort of the opposite—they just stopped caring about what I did, except when I got into trouble. At that point, they just kept trying to send me away all the time, to summer camp, to my grandparent's house in Idaho, to school extension programs, and then they just let me go anywhere on my own, with my friends or whatever, so long as I wasn't at home, in their hair."

"About how old were you then?"

"When I started the fire?"

"Okay, yes, with the plastic skull."

"I had just turned sixteen, I remember because my hair was real long at the time."

"You mentioned you got arrested once for marijuana. We're you frequently out using drugs?"

"Well, my friend was the one with the bag of weed and I was just along for the ride, but unfortunately, we got busted in his car while smoking a joint. So yeah, I was smoking it sometimes—probably no more or less than most high school kids, but I was not a big partier and beer drinker like the jocks and stuff. Some of the kids at my school were doing a lot of cocaine and using opium, taking LSD, whatever, but I wasn't really part of a drug scene like that. My friends were mostly a mix of oddballs and loners—if that makes any sense, you know, like punks, nerds, hippies, and stuff like that. I mean we were loners but we also all got along and sort of banded together."

"Did you have any best friends in high school?"

"I had a few, but it seems like we all went our separate ways once we graduated. Some of them are married already, with kids."

"Did you have a girlfriend?"

"In high school? I had like two in four years. They were cool. I miss the last one a little, but she started to get real clingy in the end, and I knew I needed my own space, so when I bailed for Hawaii, we sort of lost touch."

"Do you think she would say you dumped her?"

At that, his face grew strained and he rapped his fingers over the table repeatedly, *ker-da-thump! ker-da-thump! ker-da-thump!*—at length answering, "I never thought of it that way, but I don't know, I just have no idea. Women can be so needy, and I know I'll just disappoint them."

"Why do you think that?"

"Because I'm still trying to get my own life together, and don't want to mislead them into thinking we can have some sort of grand future together."

"So you want to focus on yourself now, to get off on the right footing before you commit to others, does that sound about right?"

"I guess so. I've never put much thought into it, but I'm just not in a very stable position right now, or doing what I want to do. A girlfriend is just excess baggage at this point, to put it bluntly."

"It's okay—I understand, but tell me, is there anyone who you feel you can really relate to now, or who is close to you?"

He shook his head, confiding, "Not here, not now. I just don't have time for that. Well, I do have a friend in Sonoma who I grew up with. We talk on the phone sometimes. He wants to come out and visit, but we're both so busy, we haven't been able to make it happen."

"Well, maybe you should—it sounds like a good idea. How often do you talk?"

"A few times a month, I guess."

"What's his name?"

"James—James Hopkins. He owns a shoe store called Concrete Jungle, at Railroad Square in Santa Rosa; sells a lot of Doc Martens. I think he has a direct contract with their distributor in England."

"Cool. I remember those shoes before Sketchers copied them."

"Exactly, and now Sketchers are the big hit while real Docs are hard to find."

"Well, they've always been sort of underground, from what I recall."

"Yeah, pretty much," he chuckled.

"Well then, I wish your friend the best of luck with his business. And what about your mother? What was your relationship like with her, and how often do you communicate with her now?"

"My mom, I think she always was hoping for more from me, like my dad, and I always substandard in her eyes. My parents are really into class image and all that—you know, keeping up with the Joneses, being the cream of the crop—and I was just there, screwing everything up. I mean, my mom started me off on piano lessons and stuff—hired a private tutor for me a few times, trying to get me to excel in school and fix my behavior, but I just was not fitting into the mold like my siblings, and I think she holds a grudge against me for that. She wishes I would become a lawyer or newscaster or something like that—anything other than what I am now, or what I want to be. She emails me a lot, and I sometimes see them for Christmas, but she still complains about me all the time, like, 'Why are you so tired all the time? What are you doing with your life? When are you going to finish college? Blah blah blah . . .' So I guess I brush her off a little; I mean, she doesn't know what it's really like trying to make it on your own, and I just don't have time to constantly fess up to her. But in the end, I can see it now—she never tried to protect me from my dad. She would always say afterward, like when he really hurt me, 'just forget it ever happened, and tomorrow you can start fresh.' But it was too late to just forget like that, the damage was done, and so, well, I've just moved on and am trying not to bother them anymore."

"It sounds like you feel your parents never really valued your path, and maybe you are right."

"No, it's just that I was a total screw-up, and how can you value that? I'm just not like them, is all—no matter how hard I try, they are never satisfied."

I could see he was becoming increasingly vexed by our conversation, with his responses becoming desultory and paradoxical. This is the point where new patients often clam up or storm out, so I diffused the air, continuing less intensely, "Okay Chris, well let's just forget about all that for now. Just sit back and relax, have a sip of water. I'm really just here to chat about *you* and how things are going with you in Hawaii."

He took a sip of water, and then started scanning the office walls again, beginning to relax a little.

"Tell me, Chris," I continued more personally, "what do you value most about *yourself* and *your* work?"

"Well, I guess . . ." he began, rubbing his chin in thought, "I'm pretty much always on time, and always try to do what is proper. I get up at o'dark-hundred' and work all day in two jobs, serving customers. I leave the house at 5:15 a.m. and get home about midnight, six to seven days a week. I try to pay all my bills; actually I and am actively seeking a third job, applying wherever I can. I've already applied to forty-three places online, even dishwasher jobs; I have a list. I take college classes, too. Even though I've been in college for six years and am nowhere near graduating, I haven't given up or dropped out. I'm just trying to do what is right and proper, you know, one must remove oneself from the equation and serve others. I've always been terrified of not having a job and not being able to support myself. Okay, like, I'm just a normal person like everyone else, trying to make ends meet. I just need to work harder, that's all."

"What are some of these bills you have? Your overhead seems pretty low for Hawaii, and you don't own a car, right?"

"No, I haven't had a car for a long time. I have a lot of debt, though. I've had a ton of dental work done since I left LA. About a dozen fillings, a lot of crowns, and three root canals, all of which I had to pay for out-of-pocket. I have some college debt, too, and a lot of debt from credit cards. But the worst one I have is a twelve-thousand dollar debt from a loan I took out about three years ago that I defaulted on and I now owe a collection agency. When I first moved here, I was really struggling, so took all the offers I could. Well, it took me a while to get on my feet here, and even though I've shaved my existence down to a minimum and have been working multiple jobs for several years, the interest penalties coupled with the ever higher cost of living has got me pretty much just treading water at this point. My biggest loan—the one that defaulted—well, I received a court order to settle it, so I called the loan officer to request a little more time to meet my next payment, citing my current hardship, and he told me, 'okay—agreed, no need to show up at court because I will drop the case for now,' but then he turned around and went to the courthouse anyway, and since I wasn't there, he won by default, and so now I also have to pay his legal fees, as well."

"That was really underhanded of him."

My patient glowered sullenly, shaking his head in remorse. "Well, it was my fault for taking out the loan to begin with."

"If you want," I entreated, "I can help look into a debt consolidation agency. Maybe we can refinance it and bring the interest rate down."

"Thank-you, sir, but I'm not sure if it will lower the monthly payment or just bulk it all into one bigger one."

"We can look into it."

He did not answer, so I moved on: "What you like to do outside of work?"

"Well, when I first moved here, I used to like to go down to the beach and swim, but I have no more time for that. And I used to like to play the piano, or read a good book, but I have no time for that stuff, either."

"Yes, of course, working two jobs and all. But how are you sleeping these days?"

"I crash pretty hard when I get home, and wake up super early, but it's just enough, I guess. I really don't sleep very much—maybe thirty hours per week, more or less."

"That's not nearly enough, Chris."

"I'm doing my best, sir . . .er, Steven. I don't really deserve more sleep than that."

"I think you do, given all that you do. Tell me, Chris, do you feel excited by stuff in your life?"

"My own inclinations outside of work have no relevance, doctor. One must work, one must do good, and one must be always in the service of others. One must not seek comforts and pleasures, nor must one exhibit or speak any type of suffering or wanting. One must cheerfully do what is right and endure with a smile any hardship. The attention must always be outward on serving others and doing good, and never on oneself, unless it is to negate one's own existence with modest words."

I was taken aback by his sudden third-person point of reference, *one* this and *one* that. He seemed to be using that as a psychological tool enabling him to bear his current predicament of working around the clock, and in dealing with a deeply wounded self-opinion, courtesy of his formative childhood experiences. I was under no illusion as to the severity of his plight, and sensed I had found him just in time. But for now, for a guy said to be so "elusive," Chris was making excellent progress on intake, and so I kept up the formal inquiry, seeking to gather as much raw data as I could while he, for whatever reason, had decided to open up to me.

"Are there any particular choices in your life you have been struggling with, past or present?" I asked.

"I was a wayward youth, and acted wrongly all the time, made all the wrong decisions. I am guilty of being a libertine, and have nothing to say for myself other than I deserve to be extinguished, like the end of a smoldering cigarette pressed against a wall. Sometimes I think that, once I pay off all my debts, that I should get rid of all my belongings, even the clothes I am wearing, and just quietly end myself, just disappear off the face of the earth and not be a bother to anyone anymore. I heard a guy did that in Christchurch recently."

"New Zealand, really?"

"That's right; nothing for anybody to hassle with or clean. He just emptied his apartment off everything, sent off his last rent check, and checked out, if you get my drift."

"I'm afraid I do, Chris. But let's not rush to conclusions like that about your life. I know you refuse to accept it, but I can assure you, you are not a bad person, and you deserve a lot more than that. You haven't killed anyone, have you?" I asked in jest, just to make a point.

He shook his head. "No."

"Okay, good—let's set a base rate we can work from then. On a scale of zero to ten, how content are you with your life?"

"Like I said, my own self, my own inclinations are irrelevant. I'm just a normal person, like everyone else—working, going to school, doing what is proper, and so I would say five—nothing too great and nothing too terrible."

"That's not the answer I was hoping for, Chris. By the sound of it, I think you rate your present satisfaction with life as closer to zero. You should know that I am here to help you, and we will keep working on it. I will not give up on you, young man. I know how low you must feel after all you've been through, but I also sense you're fighter and haven't given up on yourself, so forget this normalcy stuff—it's a myth, nobody is normal. And I'll tell you, the ones who seem 'normal' are often the most fragile people in society, the ones most at risk of crumbling if they ever had to go it alone, such as you do. So hang in there, Chris—you are a lot stronger than most, and we can get things on track for you for the long term, as in, the rest of your life, but it starts by being honest about your present unhappiness and how we can fix it."

"Happiness is overrated," he countered. "It is better to seek truth, than happiness—and the truth exists in its own realm, beyond the need of human emotions."

"That's a good start, Chris—but the truth can be grievously affected and altered by our emotions, and I think that's the crux of the problem you might be struggling with."

He regarded with that cross-eyed stare, like he were half daft and half mad. "Do you have any more questions for me?" he asked, checking his watch. "I have to be at my next job in about thirty minutes, and I've only had a banana to eat today."

"You need to get some food in you, then. Your next shift is at Hometech Hut, just down the street?"

"Yes."

"Okay, just a few more quick questions and we'll be wrapped up here. What's your favorite color?"

"Black, and yellow. But I know black is not a color."

"If you were your twin, what advice would you give?"

"Don't screw up so much; don't be such a useless shithead."

What could I say to that, in what time we had left? Chris was a real piece of work, but there was incredible hope because his direly low self-opinion also acted like a jet fuel, imbuing him with an almost superhuman drive to move beyond it, even though he currently lacked the self-worth to realize it. And so my next question: "If you didn't care about what anyone thought, what would you do?"

He rapped his knuckles twice on the desk. "Probably just play piano and write songs, go to the beach, but that's just a stupid fantasy—everyone has to work, and I'm deep in debt."

"Okay, two more quick questions. Are you religious?"

"No, not like other people are. God hates me and seeks to destroy me. Imagine that for a second—being hated by your creator, always on the run, always in hiding. And one thing I've discovered: every time I act on my own freewill, outside of the norm, God crushes me severely. I am nailed to this world in vain. I don't belong here, and God makes sure of that."

"Alright Chris, we've covered a lot today, but one last question, and we can save this for next time if you prefer: describe your three concrete wishes for your future."

"Three wishes? I wish to live a normal life, I wish to be out of debt, and I wish I could just erase myself and start over again."

"Very well, Chris. We have some legitimate stuff to talk about then, don't we? I'd like to schedule another meeting, how about for next Tuesday, one week from today. One hour: one to two. Same time, same place?"

"I need to get back to you about that," he replied as he got up from his chair. "I work seven days a week and have classes. I have to check my schedule."

"Okay, Chris, go get some food in you. You have my email and phone number, so just let me know by this Friday at the latest.

You know it's required of you to meet with me, for the time being. But I think we're making some progress, don't you think?"

I offered my hand to shake, which he did limply and hurriedly, replying, "I don't know—I guess. I will email you when I know my schedule."

"Make it happen, Chris—it is our duty, and I may have some very good news for you, hopefully by next week, about possibly cutting down on your insanely long work hours. Don't tell your employers just yet, but it's part of your therapy plan."

"Really?" He was genuinely intrigued. It seems I was the first one to throw him a lifeline in a very long time, and ironically, due to a crime he didn't even commit.

"I'm working on it, Chris. Here, is five bucks—there's a McDonalds across the street. Go get yourself something to eat before your next shift."

He refused the money, but I walked him to the elevator nonetheless, and the last thing I saw of him, as the door slid to a close between us, was his glancing up at me with a little twinkle in his eye.

August 21, 2013
Today—the day after Chris came to my office—I set to work on the final technicalities in securing the state funding for his "disability"—money to help him make ends meet as he reduces his work hours according to my therapy plan. I have also started to compile a list of things that he and I and could do together for one or more of our "sessions" outside of the office, which is a clinically permissible encounter when coded as 99 for "other" on his remittance advice. My shortlist now includes a trip to the Polynesian Cultural

Center on the North Shore, a hike up the Makapu'u Point lighthouse trail, and the Elvis Presley "Rock-A-Hula" retro show and luau in Waikiki—a diverse assortment of things he might not have done yet, but could possibly be interested in.

August 23, 2013
It is Friday, and my first week on Chris's case has borne fruit. The executive director took my application for targeted case management funding to the Department of Health state procurement office yesterday, and today they have emailed her back, copying me, approving the release of additional monies for Chris's respite therapy. Chris has also confirmed today via text message our meeting for next Tuesday from one to two in the afternoon. Until then, I will continue to work on transcribing our last session into this journal, from an audio recording I made of it.

August 27, 2013
Chris did not arrive at the appointed hour of 1:00 p.m., and then at 1:20 p.m. he sent me a text message reading: "So sorry but I can't make it today. Something work-related came up. Can we reschedule for tomorrow?"

I was none-too-pleased, and determined to find out more. I had already gained a state mandate to cut his work hours as part of his treatment, and did not want a tug-of-war with his employers—with him stretched in between—to become a common issue going forward.

"We had an appointment," I texted back. "What happened? Which job?"

Ten minutes went by without a reply, and so I called his cell phone, but was sent immediately to voicemail, suggesting perhaps that he was trying to avoid me. I called two more times and got routed each time, until on my fourth attempt I finally wangled success, when he picked up, saying, "Hey Steven, can you hold the line for a second?" It sounded as if he were in the middle of ringing up a sale, and then I heard another phone ring in his vicinity, with him answering with the greeting, "Beatrice's Bridal, may I help you?"

When he at length got back with me, I asked if he was at a third job (perhaps from the list he'd been keeping), to which he replied, somewhat cryptically, "It came up by surprise, so we will have to reschedule. I'm really sorry about—"

"Chris!" a nagging woman cut him off. "Hang that up and help with these flowers!"

"I got to go," he hastily told me. "I'll text later to reschedule." <click>

I did a Google search for Beatrice's Bridal in Honolulu, and found it listed on Yelp with a physical address and phone number, which I called and was bluntly greeted by the nagging woman, "Beatrice's Bridal."

"Hello, please forgive me but I am a friend of Chris and need to get in touch with him about a change in a recent assignment. I understand he works here now?"

<click!> she hung up on me straight away.

That was the last straw. I grabbed my baseball cap and wallet, then went over and informed my program's receptionist that I was going out to see a patient and would be back by three, when my next appointment was scheduled.

Beatrice's Bridal was located along a forgettable, second-rate shopping strip, a brisk walk of about fifteen minutes from my office. The first thing, and I emphasis *thing*, that came to my attention when I entered the store, was the sight of the woman who had harassed Chris over her Reclaim phone at HomeTech Hut. She came to handle me at the door, asking rather pointedly, as if I perhaps had made a mistake in going there, "May I help you? Is this for the misses?"

And then I saw Chris kneeling on the floor not far behind her, a small pile of high-heeled "pumps" set on the plush pink carpet as he cleaned the lower shoe rack with a rag.

"Is he new here?" I asked the harridan with sagging jowls.

She gave me the stink eye, and so I waved over her shoulder, saying, "Hey Chris, how's it going?"

"And who might you be?" the termagant asked coldly, Chris all the while looking up at me nonplussed and frozen with a rag in one hand and a silver-rimmed sandal in his other.

"Oh, just a friend," I replied. "Did he start just today?"

"We don't have visiting hours for employees," she reproached, "so if you're not here to buy something, there is no soliciting in my establishment."

"Ah, so you're the store owner," I replied, at which point Chris got to his feet.

She spun around and ordered him, "Get back to work cleaning the shoe racks!" and then she addressed me again, "That's right, buster—and it's time for you to leave!"

"Okay, well, I'll just stand outside the door until I can talk to him in person; it's very important, you see."

"Then I shall call the police for disturbing the peace!"

"Be my guest," I told the wicked witch of the Pacific, and then before I exited, I signaled for Chris to meet me outside.

"Just a moment, Misses Blum," he addressed her, as he came to follow me out. "I'm going to speak with him for a second, and all will be well."

She huffed at the idea, but nevertheless, she folded her arms and turned aside, allowing him safe passage.

Even before the door closed I asked him, I *required* of him: "Is this your third job? And why on earth are you working for that terrible woman from your other store?"

"I'm sorry, Doctor Meyers," he addressed me formally, and now that we were out in the light of day, he looked like shit, with sucked in cheeks, a wan complexion, and dark circles around his eyes. "I needed to be in two places at the same time, and am still trying to do it. Can we reschedule for next Monday, please?"

"No!" I answered emphatically. "Next Monday's a holiday. You need to tell me *now* what is going on here."

"Yes, sir, I'm sorry, sir. This is the bridal store of Beatrice Blum, the woman I sold the Reclaim phone to. She came back to Hometech and was still very unhappy about the handset. Even though I was able to activate it, she said the keypad was too small for her fingers, among other things. I asked her how else I could help her, and she kept complaining that I lacked training and common sense, and so I offered to be of further service to her by cleaning her house, washing her car—anything she wanted. That's when she told me she needed me to help at her bridal store, and so here I am, helping out."

"Helping out?—as in, without pay?!" I probed, aghast.

"Yes, sir, I was the cause of her unhappiness, and so it is my duty to make her happy again. But I don't want to disappoint you, either. Maybe we can sort of meet inside the store, chat while I'm working. Maybe she won't mind."

I turned my back to the nag in question, who was staring at us through the glass. I took a deep breath, and then addressed my patient calmly but forcefully, "Look, Chris, I'm not faulting your decisions, because I know they are out of your own goodwill, but I'm the one feeling slighted here, and let's not forget that our appointments are mandated by your PO. You simply *must* attend our scheduled meetings, or both of us will be in hot water."

"I don't want that, but how would you be in trouble if I have to reschedule a meeting?"

"Because your PO and my executive director will get all over my case about it, and I can only make so many excuses before you are returned to the judicial system and possible incarceration for noncompliance. Get it, Chris? I am your priority here, and trust me when I say, *I get you now*, kid—I get where you're coming from, and so we must stick to the plan. Dig?"

He gnawed on his lower lip, which was badly chapped.

"When was the last time you had a bite to eat, anyway?"

"I'm fasting," he said with a look of utter consternation, which he carried from me, to Beatrice in the glass, and then back to me again, continuing in a low tone, "but my bad, sir—I promise to make our meeting next time; I will try harder."

"You need to come with me right now and eat, Chris—just walk away. You are under no obligation to be here, but you are under full obligation to be with me at present, and that's an order!"

"I'm sorry, sir, but I can't do that right now—it is my duty to make everyone happy, and I don't want to let Beatrice down. Maybe we can just meet inside—"

"Chris!" I shook my head. "There are billions of unhappy people in the world—that is not your fault and they are not your problem; but some of them, like Beatrice here, will try to manipulate you into believing you are the cause of their woes, when in fact you have nothing to do with it. They will always be unhappy, no matter what you do, and—"

"What the hell's going on out here?" Beatrice interrupted, swinging the door open. "My employee's on shift, so it's time for your bearded ass to leave now!" She made the imaginary shape of a gun with her hand, pointing the "barrel" of her finger at my chest.

"This man needs to eat before he collapses!" I riposted. "You know this is a form of kidnapping, taking advantage of a young man like this? Are you going to let him go now, or must I call the police?"

"Bah! *He* offered to work for *me*, and *I* accepted—end of story! Now you're the one who needs to leave before *I* call the police! Come back inside, Chris, there are customers waiting!"

Chris looked back at me with a sheepish inquiry, which I returned with a grim countenance, shaking my head, *no*.

Brushing off his own indecision, he bowed his head in remorse, telling Beatrice, "Yes, ma'am, I'm coming," and then he addressed me, without making eye contact, "just text me a meeting time, sir—I promise I'll be there." And then, as I stood watching in disbelief, he shuffled back in behind the henpecking sociopath, and as the glass door closed between us, he stole a final, somber glance in my direction.

My concern had reached its peak, but I held my fist until I could make a rational decision, which ended with the choice not to intervene further at this time. I now knew who this woman was, and how she was exploiting Chris's generosity, should she attempt anything truly illegal on this day. Chris's self-incrimination was purely psychological, but in a world stacked with sociopaths like Beatrice who would be eager to exploit him, he was in constant risk of danger.

I marched back to the McDonalds near my office, where I placed a mindless, minimal order for a hamburger, side salad, and a cup of tap water. Once seated, I placed an order with Domino's Pizza over my smartphone, selecting a half veggie/half pepperoni pizza, a Caesar salad, and a liter of Pepsi to be delivered to Chris Fields at Beatrice's Bridal within an hour—the quickest delivery available. I paid for it in advance with a credit card, including the tip. I was not seeking to tempt Chris while he was fasting, but I could not know for sure if he was fasting out of free will, if he simply could not afford food, or worse—he may have been denying himself victuals due to his crippling tendency toward self-abnegation. Whatever the case, while under the draconian sway of the sadistic Beatrice today, he exhibited a worrisome physical frailty: a general stagger and slowness of reaction that, without his taking nourishment, might lead to his sudden collapse.

After taking a bite of my hamburger, I checked my Outlook calendar and then texted Chris with our next appointment: Thursday, August 29 at 9:00 a.m.—less than two days thence. This would allow him a buffer day to notify his workplaces for the necessary time off, but not enough time for him to be wheedled away from my authority any longer. I'd been thwarted today, but resolved to reschedule with him just this once, with my personal ultimatum that if he were to be somehow impeded again from our lawfully ordained sessions, I would intervene more forcefully with any and all acting parties, as was my duty.

August 29, 2013
Chris texted me yesterday that he wouldn't have to be at work until 1:00 p.m. today, and so his session was scheduled, not at my office, but, with his consent, at his apartment at 10:00 this morning, whereupon we would repair someplace more private to talk, and then afterward, I would drive him back to town with sufficient time for him to lunch before his dayshift began. While I had to reschedule a morning patient and a 11:00 a.m. meeting with two of my associates to make it happen, Chris's case had become quite urgent, and so fortunately, he acquiesced. I was keen to get into his domicile to personally investigate, without making it obvious, the real situation there, and to bond with him someplace less formal than in an office setting, such as on a beach, at a shave ice stand, or in a coffee house—all of which I knew Kailua hosted in abundance.

—m—

Traffic had been minimal going over the Pali Highway east, putting me into Waimanalo at 9:30 a.m., a full thirty minutes ahead of schedule. At Chris's apartment complex, I parked along the external portion of the carport, which extended beneath the block structure of adjoining duplexes. The building looked rather drab, with a cream paint job turning grey due to the prevalent wind and moisture of this "windward side" of the island, while blotches of black mold were visible beneath the roof's sagging eaves. The backdrop, however, was a spectacular carapace of green cliffs jutting up vertically for thousands of feet into the clouds, from where thin waterfalls cascaded down from narrow canyons on high. I was glad Chris could steal this heavenly view in whatever seconds he had to spare amid his busy schedule.

The doorbell to his apartment was missing the button, and so I rapped my knuckles on the door, which was peeling with paint. Eventually, the door propped open and a gruff voice inquired from the crepuscular shadows within, "Yeah, who dere?"

"Hello, my name is Steven Meyers and I'm here to see Chris. He's expecting me."

The door swung open further, and the manatee-like frame of stout Hawaiian patriarch appeared before me. He lit a cigarette and stepped aside. "He dat way," he said with a pidgin English drawl, "just follow da light by the window dere behind da curtain."

"Thank-you, sir," I answered as I maneuvered around his rotund belly.

"Eh, no mention, brah," he replied with a billow of smoke.

The apartment was hazy, dimly lit, and reeked of stale tobacco and moldy carpet. The foyer led to an L-shaped corridor made from jerry-rigged plywood, which skirted a living room partitioned into various subdivisions. This homebound shantytown would've been completely hidden from the light of day if it were not for a faint glow emanating from a burgundy curtain strung across the end of the passageway. The drape was gently rippling with a trade wind coming through, and beyond the cloth barrier, a trilling piano could be heard.

I poked my head through the side of portiere and glimpsed Chris seated before an upright piano situated on the threshold of a lanai, with the sliding glass door thrown wide open. As his hands glided side to side in recurring waves over the ivory keys, he gazed out over the mahogany instrument upon a glimmering sea.

The music in which he played was hauntingly beautiful, for he frequently employed his damper pedal to prolong the notes' sustain. I was so taken by his melody that I momentarily forgot what I was doing there, my presence nigh becoming a curious form of spying. It was only when he finished playing that I quietly clapped my hands.

He turned, and then offering a fleeting wave he said, "Hey Steven, how's it going?"

"Good stuff, Chris! I was a little early, but really enjoyed that melody."

He stared down into his lap. "I finally found some time to play," he replied with a sigh.

"Did you compose that song?"

"I did, actually. Who was it that let you in? Mike?"

"The Hawaiian guy," I replied. "The fisherman, I believe. Nice guy—is that Mike?"

"Oh, no—that's Sonny. He's super nice;" and then he continued in a whisper, "but he smokes like a chimney inside the house."

"I know. It's quite a drag, no pun intended."

Chris chuckled.

"Well, at least you have the lanai—and whoa! Check out the view! That's a million-dollar view at a whopping discount."

He pivoted in his seat to see, remaining silent, and then turned his attention toward a big open box, brimming with CDs. They were all the same, with his profile on the cover.

I went over and took a closer look. The name listed across the bottom read, "James Axton," with a CD title of, *Noumenon*.

"Is this you?" I asked, picking one up.

"Yes, sir," he replied, staring at the floor.

"James Axton: a *nom de plume*?"

He nodded.

The back cover, framed in matte black, depicted a stained glass window shaped like the keys of a piano, each key a different color of the rainbow, with a list of twelve songs beneath it.

"This is awesome, Chris. *Noumenon*—I've heard that word before. What does it mean, again?"

"Well, my take on it is: it's something that exists even if we aren't there to perceive it, like reality as it truly is, without our directly knowing it."

"Ah, I do recall now: because by our very subjective experience, we cannot know true reality, but only a substitute for it, sculpted by our own thoughts and perceptions."

"Yeah, something like that. One analogy is the cross, with the shaft being like a direct vertical alignment to reality, free of space and time, as opposed to the horizontal, worldly realm we find ourselves in, bound by temporal existence."

"Very cool, Chris; that's some pretty deep stuff. Where did you learn about that?"

"In my humanities class."

I procured my wallet and said, "I want to buy one. How much do they usually go for?"

"It's not all that great—the recording was kind of rushed."

"Oh, that's all right, I want to check it out anyway. How about twenty bucks?"

"Just take it," he offered. "It's nothing."

"Thank you, but no—I insist. Here, I'll leave this." I placed a twenty spot on top of the CDs in the box.

"Thanks, I guess," he replied diffidently, staring at his knees.

I procured a pen and asked if he would sign the cover insert with his real name.

He shook his head. "No, I'd rather not—it's really an embarrassment. I have two big boxes of those but am ashamed to sell them."

"Nah, it's cool, Chris, it can't be *that* bad. How about your alias then," I offered his CD along with my pen, "James Axton?"

After a moment of suspended animation with my arm outstretched, a stillness broken only by sound of crashing waves and the repetitive gusts of wind coursing in from the Pacific, fluttering his drape partition in uneven undulations, he at last relented. Withdrawn and inhibited, he fumbled open the case and signed "James Axton" across his ghastly white profile.

"Thank you, Chris, er—James Axton," I humored, "I really appreciate it."

"Yeah, it's cool," he replied with meek resignation, "I hope you like it."

Believing I had scored a success in gaining deeper access into something he truly relished and happened to be very talented at— music, I wished not to press the subject further at this time, and so offered we repair from his apartment, maybe grab some coffee and check out Kailua Beach.

Without answering, he got up from his piano bench. I suggested he bring his briefcase so that we could continue from Kailua directly into town, where I could drop him off near his workplace.

He set about gathering his personal effects.

Upon exiting his room, as we came upon the foyer we happened upon the house nutcase, Mike, who watched us from the adjoining kitchen while repeatedly smashing his spatula into a pan of eggs he was frying, by the smell of it. He carried a somber expression, with a dark look in his eyes.

"What's up, Mike?" Chris offered casually.

The psychopath did not answer, but kept staring at us while smashing his eggs.

"Let's go," Chris urged me, and we exited the front door.

I showed Chris to my car and opened the passenger door. "Watch your head," I said, as he tucked into the ingress of my Mimi Cooper holding his English briefcase tightly against his lap.

Kailua Beach was postcard-perfect, with a palm-stacked lawn leading to sugary white sands bereft of seaweed and other draff. Chris had stowed his briefcase in the boot on account of my vehicle's alarm system, leaving his hands free to carry his coffee as we took a leisurely stroll along the sun-splashed beach. The morning's king tide allowed the trade wind swell to run in over the outer reefs, providing for chest-high breakers on the shorebreak. We kept just above the high tide line, as we sauntered along the shore in our work shoes and slacks. Chris was wearing all black and had his hair slicked back, and may've been too warm save for his baggy trousers, short-sleeved shirt, and large iced coffee. Now and then, a larger breaker rolled in, whereupon we stopped to marvel at the bodyboarders who positioned themselves in the wave's very tubing.

"Do you like to go surf riding?" I asked.

"I used to like to bodysurf," Chris said, "and take long swims in the ocean, but I don't have the time for that anymore."

"Yeah," I sympathized with a sigh, "I know how it is. I guess we have to make time, just get up earlier and go before work. But I know you're working way too much as is, Chris. We've got to do something about that—calibrate your schedule so that you gain some of your life and passions back."

He took a rote swig of coffee, and then replied, "'Work is my life now, until I'm out of debt."

"I don't think we're ever really out of debt," I countered, "but in the meantime, our lives are passing us by."

We paused again to watch another set come in. The third wave was rather large and seemed to double up over itself, whereupon an intrepid bodysurfer cut headlong down into the curl as the entire ocean appeared to spill over the crest, detonating into the shallows with a thunderous report of exploding whitewater. The waterman emerged in knee-deep water with his trunks falling down, so he summarily yanked them back up over his gleaming skin before diving beneath another oncoming breaker. The spectacle brought something to mind which in any other setting would have been rather brash of me to inquire:

"Hey Chris, what's up with that nude swimming citation you got at Waikiki Beach?"

He regarded me with an air of surprise. "Oh, Sans Souci Beach," he replied. "That was pretty lame. When I lived in Kaimuki, I used to go jogging there in the morning before work, and would sometimes go for a dip afterward. Well, this one morning, I forgot to wear my Speedos beneath my sweatpants. I was sweating like a dog and the sun hadn't even come up yet—it was still first light, you know, so I quickly removed my sweats and jumped in near the Natatorium to cool off. But then suddenly, a bunch of other swimmers arrived and we're just sort of hanging out where I'd left my pants—they seemed to be gathering for a race or something. Eventually, I had to come in, so I made a break for my sweats. I was totally in the nude when I struggled to pull them on, and they were all laughing as I fell back on my ass into a sandy, corndogged mess. But then there was this obsessive cop watching from the showers. He marched down with an indecent exposure citation for me to sign. "Next time," he advised, "go to Dillingham and keep it under wraps."

"Good ole HPD," I chuckled. "They're very helpful after the fact."

"What do you mean?"

"Oh, nothing. They're just doing their job, but sometimes they harp on locals. Maybe you should've acted like a dumb tourist."

Chris grinned.

We continued along the breaker line, sipping our coffees and talking in fit and starts, hitting upon Hawaii politics, sea turtles and sharks, when suddenly, he stopped and said, "I shouldn't be here—I have too much to do. I know I'm in trouble, sir, and that's why we're here, but I need to be getting back to work now."

"You have until one o'clock, right?"

"Yes, sir."

"You still have plenty of time, then. But come—let's head back to the car."

We did an about face toward the parking lot, and as we advanced, I continued, "You know, our last session was more formal, where I was just asking you a lot of questions, but today we've freed up some time to figure out what you really like to do, and I think it's bearing fruit. You enjoy playing music, you enjoy exercising in the out-of-doors, and you enjoy the humanities—in fact I think you excel in these things. But you have gotten yourself in a bind of past debt, and I'm not only referring to financial debt. You carry an extra burden: you feel you have a debt to pay to yourself and the world. This, above all other things, is what's holding you back from living your full potential, from having true freedom of choice and happiness. But the first step is for you to accept that you're not to blame for everything bad that happens in the world—you only *think* you are because you weren't given proper encouragement as a child, but I am here to tell you, Chris, that there's nothing wrong with you, and that you owe it to yourself—and no one else—to live the fuller life I know you are capable of."

He shook his head and tightened his lips in a show of disappointment, perhaps at himself, perhaps at me for believing in him like that, or for psychoanalyzing him during what was beginning to feel like a simple stroll among friends. Whatever the case, his silence in the face of my assertions lent credence to their truthfulness, for otherwise he surely would've refuted me.

—⁓—

Back in my car, winding over the Pali Highway, Chris asked if I had family here in Hawaii or if I was married, to which I replied that I was unmarried and without children. "Why is a guy like you still single?" he asked.

"Like me? What do you mean?"

"You are so professional and well grounded."

I smiled. "Thank-you Chris, but my career has been my focus, and I guess I just haven't met anyone yet who has changed that, or could deal with that."

"Do you ever want to have kids?"

I glanced over at him, and then answered, with my eyes on the road again, "I would love nothing other than to have a son like you, Chris—that would make me very proud." I turned up the Hawaiian music so as not to embarrass him with such a strong sentiment. But I meant it.

Over the mountains and heading back into Honolulu proper, I relayed the good news about having secured funding to help Chris pay his bills, so that he could curtail his long work hours for a few months while we continued our sessions. He was nonplussed, contending he wasn't sure how his bosses would take a request for a reduction in hours. I replied I could provide a "medical reasons" affidavit, which they, by law, would have to honor for a period of up to twelve weeks under the Family/Medical Leave Law, or FMLA, if they knew of it or not, lest they face a legal complaint by the Department of Labor. Our only requirement would be to inform his employers five days before his medical leave was slated to begin.

He didn't reply either way if he was willing to try it, and so I forced the issue by claiming that he must, because I already had some more special sessions planned, like a possible trip to the Polynesian Cultural Center, or a hike to the Makapu'u Lighthouse—or whatever he felt like doing. Our sessions were open, I said, and were simply meant to give him a break. "Respite," I added, was the formal name used by military and medical sectors alike. Finally, he nodded his head and latently indicated he was onboard by saying he wouldn't mind a trip to see the big waves on the North Shore, such as at Pipeline.

"For sure we can do that," I said. "I heard on the radio that Kauai was already seeing some big waves from the northwest, like the wintertime stuff. I'm sure we can catch some of that action here pretty soon, too."

"I don't deserve this, sir." Chris backtracked a bit. "But, okay, if that's what you want to do."

"That's what *we* want to do, Chris, and please, I'm cool with 'Steven.'"

"Yes, s—Steven,"

I dropped him off in the Ala Moana district, at a Subway sandwich franchise near his job. As he was exiting my car, he went to close the door, but then opened it again and said, "Thank you, Steven—I'll await the doctor's slip to give my employers."

"All right!" I threw him a shaka. "You got it, Chris."

Watching him hasten into the eatery, I took a long, deep breath. I'd gotten through to the beat-up, elusive kid, establishing a bond more as a friend than as a professional, as had been my goal for this session. He was sure to lapse and be manipulated by those around him, but now I was fully prepared to enforce the legality of our endeavor with tools such as the FMLA: rights he was now aware of, should resistance arise from his employers that would force further judicial intervention. Chris was actually not a tough case to crack. We only needed some time to ourselves, away from the daily demands of the world, and today we practiced how to make it happen.

On the drive to my parking space, located at a Buddhist temple not far from my office, I listened to Chris's CD, *Noumenon*, and was deeply moved, almost haunted by the first melody, entitled, "Graven Image."

September 3, 2013

It is Tuesday. Yesterday, a Federal holiday, I texted Chris: *Tomorrow I can give you the physician's slips to give to your employers. I can meet you at the Starbucks near your morning job before your shift. Just tell me what time works best for you.*

He responded at around midnight with the message: *Not sure if I can make it. I'm in Aiea right now. I was sent to the Hometech Hut here to shut down the registers because the workers here forgot, and I just missed the last bus home. They are operating on holiday schedule tonight.*

I replied: *Why did you have to go? You don't even have a car. Are you getting paid at least?*

No, he wrote, *my boss asked me to do it and I said ok.*

Wow, I thought, *just wow*. Chris had been wheedled into bussing all the way from Waimanalo to Aiea late on a Monday night in order to amend for the mistake of workers from a satellite store, when presumably any one of them or his boss had a vehicle in which to do it themselves. This is what bothered me most about Chris's life predicament: he was an easy pushover in a world filled with people who were all too eager to exploit him. It was simply wrong, but would never stop unless he gained a modicum of self-worth.

I'm going to walk home, he texted before I could respond to his last message, *so I'll have time to prepare for my shift in the morning. I'm wearing sweatpants and flip-flops. Maybe we can meet during my lunch break between jobs.*

I texted back that I would pick him up and drive him home, because that was too far for him to walk (a distance of thirty-one miles over a high mountain range). But the receipt confirmation clock just kept spinning, suggesting he lost reception or his phone had been turned off.

After another fifteen minutes of trying to send a message but not getting through, I threw on some clothes, grabbed a cold bottle of water and went to pick him up in my car.

I drove back and forth along highways H3, 83, 61, and 72 for three hours before finally giving up the search. There was just too much space to look in the dark, too many foot trails at the side of the road and through the jungles adjacent. I thought to perhaps wait at his apartment, but decided instead to call him in the morning at about 6:00 a.m., when I estimated he might arrive back home. It was possible that his cell phone battery had died during our exchange, and that's why he ceased replying.

—⟐—

I began phoning Chris again in the morning, but to no avail, so I proceeded into my office, where I called his workplaces a few hours later. After he did not show up for either of his scheduled shifts, I spoke with Sue Tamura about it in her office. She seemed more concerned that I was unable to control my patient than by his sudden disappearance, claiming my respite therapy approach may have been backfiring, as sometimes happens when patients under occupational stress first get wind of the idea and so "jump the gun" and just stop showing up for work, believing the physician's slip would work retroactively in their truancy. In the end, I could not deny Chris may have succumbed to such a liberating assumption, given his endless work cycle punctuated by an all-night trek through the hills. In all likelihood, he had simply tossed his battery-depleted phone beside himself on his mattress and crashed out for the day with a smile on his face.

Sue, in a lilt that seemed to endeavor to embarrass my handling of Chris's case, suggested I contact his PO or even the police if I suspected a disappearance in the formal sense. But I knew that if Chris had merely botched my respite therapy plan and was at home sleeping in lieu of being at his scheduled workday on account of it, it could potentially steer him further out of my aegis by incurring a vote of no confidence regarding my methodology of keeping him "adaptive" to the common, socially accepted environment, which required his either showing up for his scheduled work shifts or calling in sick. As such, I had no intention of notifying additional authorities at this time, and kicked myself for ever having had notified Sue so soon, as her style was very corporate and exacting in the sense that her managerial defaults were more policy regimented in contrast to an underling's penchant for "thinking outside of the box," such as was mine. Thus, I told her, "No, I can handle this for now."

She cryptically rejoined, "I sure hope so."

Suffice it to say, I conveyed myself out of her office with all due haste.

—⁓—

My initial concern about my subject was not so easily subjugated by the rote assumption of Sue Tamura. I still needed to be sure Chris was okay, and furthermore, I had to get him the physician's slips ASAP if he was, in fact, already skipping out on his employers on my behalf. *All could be swiftly rectified*, I thought, *if I could only get in touch with him.* Phoning and texting him all day had gotten me nowhere, while a final call to Hometech Hut at 6:00 p.m.—a full ninety minutes after his schedule shift—evincing he still hadn't shown and was *incommuniqué*, prompted me to drive again over the hill to look for him at his apartment.

Due to some lingering traffic associated with a rush-hour accident, when I finally arrived in Chris's neighborhood, darkness had descended, rendering the crowns of the coco-palms invisible save for where the LED streetlights illumed their undersides in sepia relief. I had refrained from engaging my vehicle's headlights, riding out the twilight by my own bullheaded contrivance that I was still somehow beating the clock, block-by-block.

Suddenly, in the hue of a streetlight ahead, I saw a man with a hefty black bag hoisted over his shoulders crossing the road in front of Chris's complex. As he appeared aloof to my approach,

I kept cruising past to investigate instead of pulling into Chris's driveway. He never turned to see me, but I could tell from behind, due to his baggy slacks, bony elbows and oppressed gait, that it was my patient.

I rounded a short, curving berm in the road, then pulled over, and killed the engine. Spying on Chris at this juncture, now that he regarded me as something of a friend, I knew was an ugly proposition, but then I realized, should he catch me in the act, I could feign like I had merely come over to check up on him—as was precisely the case. Thus, the opportunity being failsafe, I exited my vehicle, shut the door in a firm but quiet manner, and then hastened on foot back to where I'd seen him crossing earlier.

I just caught sight of him as he proceeded down a palm-fringed path leading toward the ocean. The bag he carried over his shoulder appeared to be a large, black, Glad-style trash bag, stuffed with a bulky form.

I began to question more seriously something that hitherto seemed a peculiarity: why was it that Chris, a misdemeanor recidivist, was assigned to a probation officer and not kept under court probation instead? Was he a felon for a far more serious crime that was being kept a secret from me and my department? Might there be a court order of confidentiality due to some unknown extenuating circumstances? Has Chris pleaded guilty to something truly grievous? Tonight, my suspicion had become a terribly compelling force as I shadowed the mysterious oddball into the groves.

As we continued further away from the street, it became so dark that I could barely make him out as he advanced, but it was clear he was keeping to the footpath. At times I completely lost sight of him, and so I continued as quietly as my hurried footsteps would allow, fearing that if he had stepped off the path, he could just as well be watching me from the cover of jungle as I passed. I became so focused on the surrounding foliage that I stepped directly into a thick mud puddle on the path, but there I could discern fresh footsteps just starting to mend in the swampy sedge.

Continuing forward, the ground firmed up again, and soon the dense foliage on my either side opened to a purview of the seascape at twilight, with a narrow pier or raised walkway extending out over the water, whereupon Chris could be seen, carrying his hefty bag.

I continued my clandestine pursuit, shadowing at about thirty meters behind him over the dock. A thin, crescent moon was just rising over the Kaneohe promontory, casting a frail glimmer over the bay waters. My eyes having better adjusted to the dark enabled me to discern, in the wake of Chris's muddy footsteps over the floorboards, a dully glistening trail of blood. I stopped dead in my tracks, suddenly desiring more distance from my deranged patient.

Moments later, he, too, stopped walking, and then dropped his bag upon the soggy timbers with a weighty *thump!*

I began to reverse as inconspicuously as my frightened baby steps would allow.

My patient opened his bag, and then reached over and lifted a large stone or brick from the dock and placed it inside the sack before tying it shut again.

I had just jumped off the side of the pier, onto the sand, when he turned around to investigate. I stood there, frozen stiff in a semicrouch beside the wood pilings, as he seemed to be watching me. Sweaty beads of stress began issuing from my forehead. But Chris did *not* appear to see me, for he went about his secretive deed; and, exhibiting a great effort of heavy lifting, he gave his laden-down sack one hobbling swing and toss over the floorboards, where it splashed into the sea. Chris remained there for a moment, apparently watching to make sure his contraband would sink, and just as he turned to head back, I ducked under the pilings.

Thump! Thump! Thump! came my unsound patient's footsteps as he advanced, while my heartbeat seemed to beat just as loudly in my chest.

Suddenly, Chris stopped directly over me. I held my breath, struck with a profound terror that he might get to his knees and peer over the side, or otherwise jump off the pier and catch me by surprise; but to my immense relief, he kept walking toward the trailhead that had delivered us to this terrible nightscape.

I waited, and then waited some more, until I was doubly sure he was well out of sight and earshot, before I hopped back onto the pier and beetled it over the floorboards, soon arriving to a horrific sight at the end of the sea-borne loggia. There upon the sodden timbers was every evidence of murder, with Chris's bloodied footsteps impressed in chaotic patterns of evil all about the bloodstained markings left by the terrible sack he had jettisoned overboard.

I peered over the edge into a wine-dark, crepuscular moon sea, seeing nothing. I got to my knees and looked closer, when without warning, some manner of sea creature splashed my face, causing me to launch back in terror upon the bloody quagmire.

I returned to my feet to regain my wits and take stock of the situation. Concluding that it'd most likely been a small fish that had startled me, I reached over the dock again and washed the blood from my hands.

I looked back toward the phantasmagoric, black shadows of undergrowth lining the beach beneath the barely distinguishable palm trees, and grew morbidly fearful that Chris would soon return, forcing me to deal with him at that dark and isolated terminus with my back against his deathly dumping grounds. But then, the sense of duty overtook me—a duty equally to my patient as to justice, because I knew that if I reported the incident to the police, *everything* about our work would drastically change—and what if I was wrong? What if that was not a bag of human remains he had so furtively disposed of? Looking down into the wine-dark sea once more, the idea struck me as horrific, that I might jump into that somber night ocean without a mask or torch to get to the bottom of Chris's deed, but I knew I had to—and would have to quickly, before the sharks of the Pukakukui Channel sniffed the blood and would make their way in through the fringing reef to investigate, destroying all evidence and any chance I had at discovering my patient's clandestine activity. With this realization, a longing to discover the truth overcame my fear of the unknown. Thus, I stripped off all my clothes, placed them in a pile away from the bloodstains, and then jumped off the side of the pier, into the black.

Bobbing there, I took a deep breath and then dove headlong into zero-visibility that was horrific in every way. In addition to the very real possibility of large sharks being attracted to the blood in the water, I had no idea how far the bag had sunk, what sort of bottom in might have settled on, or what manner of horrors might be seeping out of it. My intense fear was accentuated further when my arm sideswiped an errant spike of jagged rebar, and I grew petrified that my face or eyes would summarily be impaled on similar construction detritus at the pier's foundation. But no sooner than this though occurred to me did my hand push into what felt like a large air bubble at the top of a sunken bag. I grabbed it in my fist and twisted my wrist, then fought for the surface, when suddenly, it became snagged on some unknown feature below. I tugged the bag ever more adamantly from one side to the other as the air in my lungs was quickly losing its sustaining power, until at last, the bag broke free, and by great effort of stroking with one hand while kicking my feet, I was able to breach the surface without dropping it.

As stars swirled before me on account of my oxygen-deprived brain nearing blackout, I grabbed a hold of the dock's rim with my free hand, and waited there for a moment to catch my breath as the creepy black sack weighed ever heavier on my other extremity. It appeared the air bubble in it was the only thing that had enabled me to wrest it to the surface, and now that the air was escaping from new holes rendered to the sack in my struggle with it, I was being rapidly stretched to the limit.

With a penultimate, teeth-gritting effort, I stretched the top of the bag between the wood planking above, and then looped it around there, providing enough staying power to allow me to clamber back up onto the pier, from where I put in one last Herculean effort, hosting the sack up over the floorboards, where it broke open with the last of my attempts.

I was too scared in that semidarkness to look back, assuming perhaps chunks of body parts and maybe a severed head would be seen there, spread out over the dock, the very eyes of the horrible cranium staring at me through tangled wet locks of brackish black hair.

You could imagine my surprise then, and a sudden ease of agitation as I glimpsed back though the gloam to perceive not the offal of a slain hominid, but dozens of plastic CD cases littering the mooring. I picked one up and focused through the star-studded night to discern Chris's silhouette on the cardstock inset.

I exhaled in shame, dragging a hand over my salty eyes and stretching my jowls long beneath my chin; shame, that I ever took sweet but troubled Chris for a psychopathic murderer, and sorrow, that he was so overcome by a dearth of self-worth that he destroyed his beautifully composed music, which was in essence his greatest outward expression.

I wiped most of the seawater from my skin with my bare hands, and then got dressed.

Further investigation revealed a photo album lying on the dock. It was already badly damaged by saltwater, but I would take it with me for further study. The mass of destroyed music I stuffed back into the holes of the punctured sack, then tied it off as best I could before tossing it overboard just as Chris had. Some CDs that wouldn't fit, I threw into the water individually, and as they appeared to half float, I became concerned someone would find them. But then again, I noticed the saltwater had permeated some of their plastic wraps, so figured by the time they might wash up onto the beach, their author would be rather unrecognizable. Yes, Chris, and now I, had committed a grievous act of pollution at Kaupo Cove, but he was clearly unhinged, and was, by degrees, taking me in that same direction. The waters surrounding the Makai Pier lied within an environmental conservatory, and so for all I knew, Chris, and now I, may have precipitated a Federal offense. I was really torn up by the event, which only strengthened my resolve to track him down for an encounter which would include stern ultimatums regarding his elusive behavior. For now, I concluded this insane escapade on the pier to be over.

But wait! I realized, as I turned to leave, *there was still one more mystery! What of the blood soaking the timberheads?*

Further investigation into the blood on the dock, glistening in the cobalt night heavens, disclosed naught but fish blood, and, as I made my way back along the pier, I discovered some offal or chum, along with the refuse of fish nets and lines, while further ashore, I came upon an area where crushed, empty beer cans had missed their mark around a municipal waste basket, above which a sign read, "Licensed Fishing between 6:00 a.m. and 6:00 p.m. only," with a city ordinance number listed. This was a popular fishing spot, apparently. I had missed the signage in my initial pursuit of Chris, but it put to rest the blood on the docks.

I marched back through the muddy coco-palm forest toward my car, shaking seawater from Chris's photo album all the while.

Back at my Mini Cooper, I stomped the mud from my shoes, and soon started up the engine and drove to Chris's apartment. I eyed my clothes for signs of bloodstains, and not finding any, I went up and knocked on Chris's door.

There was no answer, and so I knocked again a little louder.

A young Filipino-Hawaiian fellow opened the door, and he appeared to be either very tired or very stoned as he relayed with slurred speech and glossy eyes that he saw Chris coming and going about fifteen minutes prior to my arrival.

"Can you please check if he's home?" I inquired. "It's kind of important."

"*Phfft!*" he huffed. "Try wait," he relented.

As he went inside to double-check, I propped the door open further, and in the reflection of the foyer mirror, I saw the interior of my greeter's room. There was an acrylic bong with smoke still swirling around inside, and a desktop computer with a live combat game transmitting. An oversized set of headphones rested over the keyboard, and by this, I knew I'd interrupted the young man's game.

He soon shuffled back to tell me more adamantly that Chris had left the house.

"Did he mention where he was headed?"

"Beats me, brah."

"Okay, thanks," I replied as he closed the door on my face.

Back inside my car, I called and then texted Chris, explaining that I was in the area and wanted to take him out to dinner, if he'd only reply. I made no indication that I'd been shadowing him or knew anything about his CD dump.

After waiting five minutes with no response, I drove around Kailua Town looking for him, circulating through the main areas to no avail.

About ninety minutes later, I pulled into a restaurant parking lot and examined Chris's saturated photo album. It began with pictures of him as baby, cradled in his parents' arms as they cooed down at him; then there were images of his siblings, apparently, from years bygone; now he was a preteen, seated behind a piano; and then suddenly, he was a teenager, his hitherto innocent smile now turned upside down in a brooding frown. These sullen images often depicted him alone behind his piano with his head craned over the keyboard, or otherwise he was turning his back to the camera as if starting to walk away.

I shut the book and hummed a guttural groan, my heart aching over the album that Chris had tossed to the sharks. I then realized that I hadn't eaten since 9:30 a.m. I was parked in front of an esteemed local eatery called Mexico Lindo, so went in for a warm enchilada plate replete with rice and refried beans.

—◊◊—

After eating, I perambulated around the immediate area, keeping a lookout for Chris as I walked off my meal. At length, I ended up in a bar called Gaslamp, where I took a seat in the corner, ordered a rum and coke, and then procured this journal to input the day's entry. More drinks, coupled with the soothing sounds of a Hawaiian slack-key jazz trio performing in the opposite corner, kept me writing longer than I probably would have otherwise, until "last call" was suddenly announced. The establishment formally closed at 2:50 a.m., when I stumbled out with the last of the patrons a cocktail short of smashed.

September 4, 2013
I tilted my seat back and stewed in my car, about to doze off until I was I alerted by a police car blaring by. Only one other vehicle

remained in the restaurant parking lot besides mine, and sitting drunk behind the wheel, I knew I'd probably land myself in jail should the cops cruise in to investigate. Therefore, I hit the streets on foot once more, this time seeking to walk off my buzz.

All was quiet in Kailua Town save for the rare passing vehicle or distant siren. I saw one homeless person sleeping at a bus stop, and a few blocks further, I encountered another street person, judging from his grimy condition and wanton disposition. With time on my hands, I thought I'd stop to inquire with him, as he proceeded in my direction, if he'd seen the likes of Chris. He was at first taken aback by my sudden late night confrontation, and then he appeared fearful about my intentions.

"Hey bud, let me help you out," I entreated with a dollar bill, which he received with a nod of recognition. "I've been looking for a guy;" I said, "a friend of mine from around here. . . ." and then I went on to describe Chris's age, height, and general profile.

The street person nodded, answering in pidgin, "I dink da kine around here somewhere. Dis oddah *haole* guy, I ask for a dolla, and you know what, brah? He slap me a Jackson."

"When was that?"

"Shoots, brah, a few hours back."

I thanked the unfortunate local, and then went on my way while he just stood there, watching me leave. His story about asking a stranger for a dollar and getting a twenty-spot instead, frankly, it matched the rare manner of selflessness that Chris was prone to display. But with a few hours time between that event and now, I was even less inclined to believe I might still find my patient before dawn. In all likelihood, he'd long since retired to his apartment to sleep, while I'd been overreacting. This day, it seemed, was merely a day of soul-searching on his part, and soon, I was sure, he would contact me to talk about his findings.

I made a final stop at a gas station convenience store to buy a bottle of water, which I summarily quaffed down before returning to my car. While I was enervated from walking, my vision had straightened out and my reaction time had improved enough to brave the ride home without incurring a DUI, or so I surmised.

At 5:40 a.m., I turned the engine, pushed Chris's CD into the console, and headed out onto Highway 72.

As I rounded Sea Life Park, the second song, entitled "Black Rainbow," began not unlike Claude Debussy's "The Girl with the Flaxen Hair." And then, driving ever higher into a misty morning fog that engulfed the precipitous roadway, I was altogether haunted by the musical refrain.

Suddenly, the Makapu'u Point lighthouse broke through the mist in an imposing, dark castle display. The surreal imagery, coupled with Chris's poignant melody, completely overwhelmed me, and tears went streaming freely down my cheeks.

At home, I made the difficult decision to return to work and not call in sick. While I hadn't slept a wink, I didn't want to stir the boat with Sue, for I had several intake patients scheduled, two of whom she'd gone to great lengths to coordinate into our program. I reeked of rum, which I tried to dispel with a long shower and heaps of cologne. I was disappointed with myself for ever having had slipped into such a "survival mode," and resolved to sleep it off and learn from it as soon as I returned home that evening.

At work, I think the only thing that enabled me to avoid a discussion with Sue about Chris was the many other new patients I was tasked with seeing. His PO, however, sent me an inquiry via email whose timeliness raised suspicion. Did he somehow know that Chris had escaped my control? Were Chris's employers calling around, inquiring of his whereabouts? I had no way of knowing by the tone of the email, so decided not to answer until I contacted Chris. I redoubled my efforts at calling him, emailing him, and texting him in between my scheduled patients.

Toward the end of the day, Chris was still missing in action from both his jobs, while his employers had pressed me, when I called them, about who I was, exactly, and what was going on with him. I was now fully aware of how volatile and worrisome the situation had become concerning Chris's behavior, and how much a toll the case was now taking on me, as well. As such, at 5:00 p.m. sharp—the technical end of my workday—I departed the office and drove eastbound through rush hour traffic, quaffing a large iced coffee from McDonalds as I resolved to once and for all find my patient and reprimand him with a stern legal warning should he continue to remain aloof from my dictates. My vision was pressing in from the sides, with thick puffs of sleep cradling my weary eyes.

I arrived at Chris's apartment a little after 6:00 p.m. and was greeted at the door by another one of his housemates: a Filipina woman closer to my age who said that Chris had left a few hours earlier. When I pressed her for details, she said she had heard a banging sound against the wall emanating from Chris's room, and when she drew closer to listen, she heard him on the phone making a flight reservation to San Francisco (SF) for that same evening. She then saw him depart with a bloody nose and carrying an overnight bag.

I asked this woman—Esmeralda—if she could take me to his room to see, claiming I was a family friend that he may've left a missive for. She agreed and we proceeded in together.

There was a slight marking of blood on the wall, but otherwise nothing looked out of place from my last visit, save for the missing box of CDs.

"Do you know if he paid rent for September yet?" I inquired.

"I have no idea," Esmeralda replied.

"Can I leave you with my phone number, then, and if you find out he hasn't paid, just contact me about it?"

"It's better you talk to the landlord about that, because I'm too busy to get involved. I barely know Chris and he's not my responsibility, anyway."

I acquiesced, and then, opening the notes app on my cell phone, I entered the landlord's contact information she provided.

"Is that all?" she pressed. "I have to get ready for work now."

"Please, ma'am—just one more thing: do you recall which airline Chris contacted to make his flight reservation?"

"No, I didn't hear anything else about what he was doing. Now is that all?"

"Thank you ma'am," I capitulated to the flustered woman's indifference, and then she rapidly conveyed me out of the apartment, firmly shut the door and engaged the deadbolt.

My case with Chris had suddenly gone from difficult to seemingly unworkable, but I was loath to give in. It may've been that my mind was unhinged from lack of sleep, or that I refused to admit failure to Sue, or that I now felt a vested interest in Chris that went beyond my professional duty, but whatever the case, this triumvirate of recrudescing goblins got under my skin and drove me on, all the way back to the Honolulu International Airport, where I hastily parked in the first long-term garage I found and then marched into the departures terminal of Alaska Airlines—my random choice based on their frequency of SF-bound flights.

The clerk at the check-in counter searched her database of recent and pending departures, but did not find Chris Fields booked on any of the planes. She suggested I proceed to the customer service center and request a terminal-wide announcement of his name.

En route to do so, I stopped by the Hawaiian Airlines desk and inquired with the attendant there about his computer's flight logs. The truth was, part of me knew that Chris would be reluctant to respond to a loudspeaker announcement of his name because he was undoubtedly on the lam. As I began rubbing my eyes, deeply fretting over my next course of action, the attendant suddenly hit upon Chris's name.

"Yes, I see him here," he said: "Chris Fields. He checked in to flight 101 departing to SF at 5:35 p.m. and is currently en route. Is everything okay, sir?"

I thought for a moment about how best to handle the situation, soon replying, "Yes, everything is fine. But can you please tell me what time his flight is due to arrive in SF? I will be arranging a car for him."

"Certainly: he's due to arrive at 12:42 a.m. in terminal three."

I thanked the clerk for his help, and then turned to check my cell phone. I wasn't looking for anything in particular, but was only pondering what to do next without having to stand there before the attendant in awkward silence. My mind scrolled through a foggy and chimerical process of elimination. The most immediate and desperate measure would be to request a message be sent directly to Chris's plane, or otherwise to the ground crew at San Francisco International Airport (SFO). But what could I say that wouldn't cause him run faster away, or get him into further trouble? He technically was still not doing anything illegal. His PO had required his mandatory inpatient rehabilitation at our program offices, while Sue and I had attained a respite order and associated state funding for his case. But it was possible that if he returned to Hawaii within a week or so, his sojourn to the mainland could be passed off as a visit to relatives or what not. His flighty departure with an overnight bag suggested either one of two things: he did not intend to be gone for long, or he was running away for good. I had to hope against all likelihood that it was the former, because the latter—an ultimate fleeing—would prove disastrous to his criminal record and his rehabilitation under my command. I thus had no legal reason or right to request he be detained at SFO, which would require him to be put into Federal custody—way too drastic of a measure at this juncture, or so I surmised. To merely send him a note that I wished to speak with him had plainly gotten me nowhere already, and might even spur him to become even more evasive. It may be that Chris felt shame in opening up to me, and despised being analyzed and detained under close scrutiny, and so I decided not to request the authorities to interfere on my behalf.

My next option was to let him go and hope he returned before things got much worse for him here in Hawaii, and in the meantime, I would try to cover for him until he got back. But this would place too much risk, not to mention additional stress, on me. I could not continue to hide his delinquency much longer, and if we were found out, I would be in as much hot water as him, potentially losing my job for going rogue, i.e., "for taking things into my own hands" and "lying on his behalf." So, hoping and waiting were poor choices. Chris wasn't long ahead of me, I thought in my delirious and desperate state of mind, and so I resorted to the only option I still had any control over, which was chasing him down. I returned to the attendant and asked, "When is your next flight to SF?"

"There's a red-eye at 10:05 tonight," he said, "but it's fully booked."

Not wanting to risk a waiting list, I thanked him and then went back to the Alaska Airlines counter with the same inquiry, this time having better luck with a 9:55 p.m., red-eye that had several seats available in economy and first class, and so without further ado, I booked an economy-class ticket with the intention of tracking Chris down in SF or environs. I knew it was a long shot, but I felt something of the bloodhound in me and knew it could be done. The fact was, I was not altogether thinking straight, and felt committed beyond the Rubicon to track him down and save the case.

I went back to my car to rummage what I could for the trip, grabbing my workbag, windbreaker, sunglasses, *Noumenon*, etcetera.

—ɯ—

While waiting in the departure terminal for my flight out, I donned on my sunglasses to shield my darkened eyes. Sipping an iced coffee, I phoned the reception counter at my office, which I knew would be unmanned. If Sue happened to be working late and picked it up, I would summarily disconnect, as the reception phone had no caller ID feature. Thankfully, my call rolled into voicemail, as was the plan. I left a message that I would be taking a sick day tomorrow. Being in upper management with the state, that was all I was required to do. I knew it would make Sue unhappy, but I was acting within my rights. Only after three consecutive sick days would a doctor's slip be required.

The call had given me a sense of relief, and so with what time I had left before boarding, I continued to write in my journal.

At last, jetting eastward toward the mainland, I fell asleep with my journal in my lap.

September 5, 2013
The date listed above was the first thing I read, as I was awoken by a stewardess on account of our pending arrival. My journal was still open in my lap, where I had completed the previous day's entry before falling asleep with pen in hand—the writing instrument now resting on the floor between my feet.

The pilot announced preparations for landing, and once on the tarmac, "Welcome to San Francisco International Airport. It is Thursday, September fifth. The local time is 5:27 a.m., with a temperature of fifty-two degrees and overcast. . . ."

I was a full five hours behind my quarry, and even more dazed from lack of sleep than I'd been yesterday. Nonetheless, I had nabbed a few hours of shut-eye, which would be enough to carry me through the next leg of my hunt—or so I believed.

I deplaned and caught a tramcar into the city, from where I transferred to a streetcar, checking into a hotel in Fisherman's Wharf almost two hours later. My logic in pursuing Chris to this sector of the sprawling Bay Area was sketchy at best, and rather embarrassing to admit, being based solely upon a lingering sentiment I had about shadowing him to the Waimanalo pier in Hawaii. I was indeed growing delirious, while even my balance was off-kilter—the slightest bump could knock me over.

As soon as I checked into my room, I set my cell phone alarm for three hours ahead and then collapsed over the bed.

—◊◊—

I awoke late in the afternoon and regretted having had slept through my alarm, but, without doubt, I'd direly needed the extra few hours in my power nap. I exited the hotel and walked to a nearby pier that featured restaurants overlooking the water, settling on one that served clam chowder in a completely edible, sourdough bread bowl.

The heavy meal went a long way to get me grounded and restore my vigor. As I was finishing, I procured my smartphone and did a Google search for Concrete Jungle shoe store in Santa Rosa. I found the number and called it from my restaurant table, for it was almost 6:30 p.m., and I didn't want to risk missing the store's operating hours. A young woman answered. I asked for James Hopkins, the manager. She asked who was calling. I told her I was a friend of Chris Fields. She asked me to hold the line.

"Oi! This is James," the manager said with a British or Scottish accent.

"Hey, my name is Steven Meyers. I'm a friend of Chris Fields. He said that you knew him?"

"Sure, Chris in Hawaii—yeah we go ways back. Why, what's up?"

"Actually I live in Hawaii, too—that's where I met him, but I think he recently moved back to California. Have you heard from him lately? I'm trying to contact him to say hello and see how he's been doing, but I don't have his new contact info."

"Is that right? Sounds like he finally made the move, then. Good on him. The last few times we jawed, he told me he wanted to move to SF where the weather was cooler and he'd have better job opportunities. How long ago did he make the move? I haven't heard from him in a while."

"I think he moved this week, actually."

"Did you try his Hawaii number, lad? Maybe he still uses it?"

"I tried that, but I can't seem to get through. Can you do me a favor and call him—it's pretty important. He left something back in Hawaii that he probably needs."

"Alright, sure thing—I'll give him a jingle straight away."

I gave James my number, and added, "If Chris contacts you, please ask him to call me, and let me know when you hear from him. I really need to speak with him and find out where he is."

"I'll do that, lad. I've been telling him to come out and work for me, but I don't think he wants to live up here in the 'burbs. I'll try to contact him, and tell you what he says."

"Thanks, I appreciate it. How's the Dr. Martens business going, anyway? Chris mentioned that was your specialty."

"Retail can be a chore, but I enjoy having my own store. We're nicely situated here on Railroad Square, so drop in the next time you're in this neck of the woods. I'm here almost every day and will cut you a fifteen percent discount."

"Fifteen percent, nice! I'll be sure to do that, thanks."

With that, we wrapped up the call. My bloodhound intuition was bearing fruit, but still, SF appeared rife with nooks and crannies, and so I knew finding Chris would not come easily.

I sauntered to the end of the wharf, thinking of how I might better triangulate Chris's whereabouts. I was reluctant to contact his parents, believing it would be better if they weren't involved in his life any further, for they apparently had done him enough damage already, while he needed to craft a new future centered on self-esteem without their continued psychological warfare. But, I conceded, just in case Chris might contact them, I decided to try to touch bases with them, as well. As it was already three hours later on the east coast due to the time differential, I marched back to my hotel and began digging through my files for the full name of Chris's parents in South Carolina. I eventually founded them, scribbled at the bottom of Karen B.'s intake sheet.

My online search for his mother kept missing the mark, and so I ran a query for Gerald Fields, his father, and found him without too much difficulty, if the name listed for him in South Carolina proved correct. I took a swig of water, a deep breath, and then dialed the number.

"Hello?"

"Hi, is Gerald Fields there?"

"Who is this?"

"My name is Steven Meyers. I'm trying to get in touch with the father of Chris Fields."

"Why? What kind of trouble is that good for nothing som' bitch in now?"

"No trouble, sir. I'm his counselor and am trying to reach him. Are you his father?"

"Yeah, unfortunately. Where's he now? Still in Hawaii?"

"That's what I'm trying to find out, sir. He may have gone to SF on holiday, or as a permanent move."

"And so? What kind of counselor are you, anyway? A school counselor or nutjob counselor?"

"School and career counseling," I obfuscated. "I think you should know he has been doing very well: he works two jobs and is excelling in college. But recently I have lost contact with him, and so I was hoping that if he should contact you, if you could let me know his whereabouts so I can update his matriculation schedule."

"Matriculation schedule, eh? You mean he hasn't even graduated yet? How many bloody years has it been, anyway? Ten?"

In the background I heard a woman's voice, "Who is that, dear?"

There was a shuffling sound—perhaps an attempt to cover the phone receiver—followed by Gerald's reply, "Nobody, honey, just an old college buddy."

When he came back on with me, he changed his tone more amicably, saying, "That sounds good, champ. I have your number here on caller ID. I'll let you know if I hear from him." <*click*>

He hung up before I could respond. I had no way of knowing if he'd actually saved my number, but obviously, he didn't give a flying fuck about his son. My original determination to keep Chris totally sheltered from his parents going forward had just been reinforced by Gerald Fields, his father.

I was angry and wanted to blow off steam, so set off on foot again, this time in search of Chris. I'd never been to SF before, so brought up a real-time map online, from which I proceeded along the waterfront area, called the Embarcadero, en route to the city's main drag, Market Street. It seemed this was a popular promenade for tourists, who used it to access the many piers offering fine dining and retail shopping. As such, I did not expect to find Chris here, but took a glance at everyone I passed, just in case. It may've seemed like a long shot, what I was doing, but I had to start somewhere, and I now had a pretty good hunch that he was somewhere in SF, based on what James in Santa Rosa had said.

At the foot of Market Street, the whole city seemed to stretch down the wide thoroughfare in an orderly column, with cable cars and trolleys rumbling to and fro alongside sidewalks abuzz with all manner of characters, from business people who had worked late, to youngsters strolling about, to tourists and locals clutching shopping bags, to homeless people, street urchins, and cops.

I must've covered six or seven miles in this area, cruising up and down hillside neighborhoods, such as Chinatown, the Tenderloin, and South of Market. Several times, I saw individuals who somewhat resembled Chris in walk and stature, but who turned out not to be him.

My best lead came courtesy of a police officer. I'd stopped five separate cops to inquire if they'd seen a likeness of Chris, describing him as a person prone to committing Good Samaritan deeds. Two officers said they were looking for a guy who matched both my physical and character description of him, citing a "suspect" who'd been going around earlier that day distributing gift cards to homeless people.

"Is that illegal?" I inquired of one of the cops.

"Not in and of itself, but it raises some suspicion about how he's obtaining these cards and what his intentions are."

"Could it be that he's buying them and handing them out to help the homeless?" I countered. "Where are the cards from?"

"That would be a great act of philanthropy, if such is the case," this cop—Officer Tom Edwards—replied. "But the problem is, we've been getting a lot of complaints today from places like Macy's, The Gap, Subway sandwiches, and Burger King, about highly unsanitary street people going in to use these gifts cards. It's become an issue of public health and disturbing the peace. Some of our street people never shower, and their clothes are grimy with urine and defecation, and half torn off around their private parts."

"It's a very sad condition for them," I offered. "Maybe those gift cards will help to change that."

"I realize that," replied Officer Edwards, "but it's hard on these businesses, too, when their customers drop their shopping baskets and leave the establishment as soon as these others shamble in. San Francisco has a big homeless problem, did you know that? Are you from around here?"

With his inquiry, I started a slightly more personal acquaintance with Officer Edwards, revealing that I was Chris's psychologist and that my patient needed my help. I left him with my phone number to call in case he should find out more about this mysterious Good Samaritan, or if "Chris Fields" surfaced on his precinct's radar. He agreed to collaborate, and left me his number, as well.

One thing that I'd been struggling with since nightfall was a drastic cooling of the outside temperature. My lightweight Hawaii clothes and windbreaker were barely cutting it—in fact I had to maintain a brisk walking pace, just to ward off the cold.

One the way back to my hotel, I stopped in for some crab and wine at a late night restaurant in North Beach—a famous dining area. Afterward, I capitulated to my tired feet and leapt onto the back of a cable car, which conveyed me up and over the steep streets to its terminus in foggy Fisherman's Wharf, not far from my hotel.

Back in my room, I kicked off my shoes and laid upon the bed, content that my instincts had led me on the right track, and so for the first time in many moons, I fell asleep unperturbed.

September 6, 2013

Today, Friday morning, I awoke all-too-late, perhaps on account of the time change, but whatever the cause, it was already past 8:00 a.m. Hawaii time when I placed a call to my office to report in for another sick day. Alas, it wasn't sufficient enough to inform the secretary, for Sue Tamura, my boss—the executive director—had wanted to speak with me, and so I was forwarded to her almost instantly.

"You are requesting another sick day off, Doctor Meyers?" she addressed me formally. "Is everything okay?"

My mind tripped over itself for a second, until I realized I was too deep in this to keep hiding, so I wagered my case on honesty, replying: "Actually, Sue, I need to tell you that Chris Fields has gone to SF, but the circumstances surrounding his departure were so concerning that I have decided to investigate."

"Why, what happened? And what do you mean by investigate?"

"I'm in SF now, and—"

"What?! You followed a patient out-of-state?!" she was incensed, but then continued more quietly, remaining stern, "You know that's a massive breach of policy, Steven!"

"Chris may have sustained a head injury prior to his departure," I explained. "He could be suffering from amnesia, or worse."

"What kind of head injury? What happened?"

"He may have banged his head against a wall enough to draw blood from his ears. Sue, this could be serious. I only ask—"

"Wait, wait, Steven—stop right there. Whatever the case with Chris's health or injury, you're not following protocol. There are other people you should be contacting, and you know that. You missed a whole slew of intake patients yesterday, some of whom are rescheduled for today, and you're blowing off important meetings. And need I remind you, your wild goose chase out-of-state could have legal ramifications for the entire department."

"No, Sue, I do not intend to put anybody in jeopardy. Chris has become a personal challenge of mine, and I wish not to fail him, *or* my duty to the State of Hawaii. I am only asking for a few more days of sick time, or even vacation time or leave without pay if need be. Regard it as a personal trip; we need not make it a public issue."

"A few more days?!" she fired back. "It's one thing to be out for a legitimate emergency, but tending to clients in an extracurricular setting, and especially out-of-state, is *not* permitted in the use of our absence electives, if at all."

"That he has left the state," I pushed back, "does not absolve me of my moral duty to help him, since I'm the only one who's ever gotten through to him in any significant way. His life may be in great danger, and so I have vowed to help him, at least temporarily."

"You must return to Hawaii at once, Doctor Meyers!"

"But why must compassion stop at the confines of one's state capacity!?" I reiterated.

"I implore you, doctor, to return to Hawaii ASAP and not let this incident leak out, because if it does, you'll be putting me, yourself, and the entire Hawaii state section in hot water by continuing to pursue him out-of-state because the respite funds have already been delivered, and those are *Hawaii* state funds intended by law for *Hawaii* cases only, so the action you are now undertaking may very well red flag our whole operation! The Feds will audit everything from the program general fund, to our special funds, to your travel expenses and work time that you are allotting to an unauthorized out-of-state endeavor."

"Well, just don't spend any of it on my present action, then."

"It's—not—that—sim-ple, Ste-ven," she exhorted in mottled syllables. "The respite funds are already tied into the general fund pool, making it very difficult for me to prove a case of nonusage. Are you suggesting I cook the books, doctor?"

Now she'd gone too far. "Of course not, Sue! Why must you jump to such extreme conclusions?!"

"No, doctor Meyers—you're the one who has jumped to extremes in chasing your patient out-of-state. Chris is probably just skipping out on his debts. For all you know, he may be setting the system up further by feigning an injury before leaving. If he doesn't want to stay in Hawaii and face his music, Hawaii will be better off without him, believe me. God knows we have enough desperados coming here from the mainland. Our priority should be in taking care of our own first!"

"But Sue! Chris has lived in Hawaii for six years, and has been a working person of service. Does that not qualify him as local enough? His present predicament is the most severe I have ever encountered by far, due to possible head trauma. You've got to permit me to investigate for just a few more days."

"The proper course of action, doctor, is to first notify his PO here in Hawaii, who will coordinate with the SF police department and programs there, and let them handle it, because it is now out of the aegis of our mandate as a state services welfare clinic.

"I can do some of that here, on the ground, where I can be of more direct assistance in the transfer of care. In just one day here, I have already made significant headway."

She sighed disappointedly, continuing, "It is very inappropriate for a man of your professional capacity to go rogue and simply abandon so many meetings and other patients while you go flying off on a wild goose chase out-of-state; actually you are the first person that I have *ever* heard attempt such a reckless action."

I did not reply—she had her views, and I had mine.

After a moment of tense silence, she continued with subdued voice, "Okay doctor, here it is: to avoid a massive audit that would only waste more of our time and resources, I will grant you leave without pay, and quietly tell people here that you had some sudden personal business that required your hasty departure out-of-state. You can explain it as you wish upon your return, but as far as I'm concerned, the other details of this conversation never transpired."

"Very well then, leave without pay," I conceded, and then soberly repeated, in an effort to succor human sympathy, "but please remember that Chris may have suffered serious head trauma before leaving, and may be at the perils of some form of amnesia or dementia. You know how long it can take for cases like this to show up on the radar again in another state, especially in a big city like SF already crawling with homeless, and you also know that, by then, the subject in question is usually far worse off than before he left. And I'll tell you, I was able to contact his father in South Carolina, and he's a major asshole—couldn't care less about his son."

"Again," she replied in a hushed tone, "contact his PO here; tell him only that Chris has left the state, but not that *you* have left, and then only if he advises, contact the authorities in SF *by phone or computer*," she emphasized, "and then I *highly* advise that *you* return *here* to your *other* patients before things *really* get out of hand!"

"Okay then;" I acceded, but only in sentiment to appease her undue panic, "please email me the leave without pay papers—I'm sorry but I don't have any on hand. I will sign and send them back ASAP. But since I'm already here in SF, I intend to at least get the ball rolling on Chris's case, lay some groundwork for him before I about-face. Otherwise, it's a complete wasted effort."

To which she cryptically replied, "I will send the form, but for your sake, I urge you to resolve this sooner than later."

"Please do that," I said, and then with an even and cynical "aloha," I hung up the phone before she could volley another word. It was so strange working in the sector of clinical psychology while being bound to cold, corporate policies. It was because I worked for a state institution, beholden to strict state and Federal guidelines. I thought, for a moment, of what differences starting my own private practice would allow in regard to patient jurisdictions and interactions, concluding rather quickly, in a manner to spare myself my own embarrassment, that it would not serve me well to go to such lengths as I was presently doing for Chris, if he were a patient in my own business, because a disciplined professional would need to set his own limits and not go globetrotting after such highly aberrant cases. But Chris, the humble and good Chris Fields—how could I compartmentalize him as a mere client and not a friend in need? He had already made such an appreciable impression on me, and thus, I wasn't willing to let him go on suffering so summarily, as Sue had admonished I drop the case, essentially.

Seeking a more balanced perspective, I placed a call to Karen B.—his care coordinator. She was available to speak, and so I told her about my difficulties with the case, and these most recent developments.

Her reply was that she could not publicly disagree with Sue's sentiment on the matter, but that she privately wished me the best of luck in finding Chris, believing I was acting "merely out of love," which she declared was "the most proper instinct." She urged me to contact her if she could be of further assistance, and I implored her to keep these developments on the lowdown, to which she agreed, but not expressly.

The clothes I had been traveling, walking, and sleeping in these past two days needed to be changed, and so without further ado, I explored the immediate area looking for a new outfit to see me through a few more days. There were no standard clothing stores per se—only a few woman's fashion boutiques, and some souvenir stores for tourists. While these latter had a good selection of shirts, they did not carry pants.

I took a break, stopping in for a late breakfast at an Americana diner, and afterward—at the suggestion of my waiter—I went to a nearby shopping pier where I found an NFL store and a Harley Davidson clothing outlet that carried enough haberdashery between them to assemble a full outfit for the variable SF climate.

Back at the hotel, I paid for another night's stay, and then organized my scanty travel effects before taking a hot, soapy shower.

By the time I hit the streets again in search of my subject, it was already 1:20 in the afternoon. I felt a little remorseful about having fallen behind the curve time-wise, but at least I was better suited for the streets of SF. My outfit now consisted of "official" 49ers football team sweat pants and collared shirt with embroidered 49ers logo, a Harley Davidson bandana, which I wore as a scarf, and a Harley motorcycle jacket, thin and form-fitting, and purchased at a big discount. It may've been on sale because the patches on the back read, "Rolling Stones," and, "Altamont Free Rally, 1969," which I later learned was a concert attended by the Hells Angels, whose member Alan Passaro stabbed a man to death when Alan saw him pointing a revolver in the air toward Mick Jagger on the stage.

Whatever the case, for the time being, my new attire permitted the ease of movement I required while not sacrificing warmth in the varying SF clime. Should my stay in the city be prolonged, I would simply avail myself of the hotel laundry service, every other day.

To continue my search, I caught a street trolley to the downtown area that Chris was thought (by the police) to be operating, disembarking at the Embarcadero transit station and continuing on foot up Market Street, from where I wove both "south of Market" and up into the Tenderloin district.

It seems I'd lain my eyes upon the full panoply of humanity, from well-heeled museum-goers to the most destitute of homeless, but in the broader swath of regular Joes where I hoped to find Chris, I was beginning to grow doubtful I would ever see his elusive countenance. Resigning to a late lunch at a Subway sandwiches outlet to rest my feet and rethink my game, a big break in the case finally came. Officer Edwards had texted from his local precinct, citing "an issue of great importance" for which he required my presence at the police station as soon as possible.

I Google searched the location and texted back: "I'll be there in fifteen minutes."

—៚—

"There's some CCTV footage I want you see," Officer Edwards revealed from the confines of an internal office. "I think it may be our man. It was captured earlier this morning and matches the suspect in yesterday's gift card case, based on CCTV footage recently obtained from stores that were able to positive ID the card numbers being sold to the suspect in question. Only today's incident is far more grave."

I regarded Officer Edwards with a concerned expression.

"This was captured from the concourse of a hotel at the foot of Nob Hill, near the Tenderloin."

He ran the clip, which depicted a man stumbling around a corner while holding his bleeding stomach. He collapsed near the concourse, where bystanders appeared to scream, and then others rushed to his assistance. Moments later, another man was seen rounding the corner while brandishing a bloodied piece of steel. He was dressed in Hawaii business casual, with khaki slacks and a floral patterned, stonewashed "aloha shirt," but his clothes were slightly matted and soiled. He stopped before the terrified onlookers, and then appeared to say something before dropping his weapon and running away.

"I think that's him!" I exclaimed as the loop started over. "I think that's Chris Fields! What the hell has happened?! Can you give me a close up?"

Officer Edwards replied, "The man who fell down had been stabbed in the abdomen, and was dead on arrival at the hospital. Another victim was found stabbed to death around the corner. The suspect seen in the footage, who we believe is Chris Fields, is holding one of the murder weapons. Eyewitnesses report him saying, 'I'm sorry for what I have done,' before he fled. He is now wanted as a person of interest on suspicion of murder."

As he spoke, he froze the frame and then zoomed in on the suspect, who was several days unshaven and looking rather derelict, but the semblance to my patient was indubitable.

"Jesus," I gasped. "It *is* Chris Fields, I can tell you for certain—unless he has a twin brother, which I don't believe he has. Is there any footage of the actual stabbings around the corner? Were there any witnesses?"

"We're still searching for leads. Crystal methamphetamine was found on the other victim, while the guy fallen here had a pocketful of cash paper clipped into neat bundles. It looks like a drug deal gone bad. What's your take of Chris's involvement in this?'"

"I think you must know, officer—and I'm telling you truthfully, that Chris has a record for taking the blame for other's crimes."

"A police record?"

"You know I'm his psychologist from Hawaii," I reminded. "I tracked him here two days ago after he skipped out on our therapy sessions and left his jobs without notice. He suffers from extreme low self-esteem, and may have suffered head trauma just prior to his leaving. Please tell your other officers to go easy on him—he may be completely innocent. This needs to be investigated further to find out what really transpired."

He regarded me critically, and then said, "I will need to take a report from you, which may be submitted before a court of law. When we do catch this Chris Fields, depending upon how the case develops, you may be called to the witness stand to submit further testimony."

"Yes, absolutely, I will do it."

"Let me ask you, off the record, do you think he was capable of this heinous act?"

"No, not as I knew him, but if he is suffering some form of brain damage, now, well—I just don't know. We cannot know anything until we find him."

"Let's get to that report, then, so I can return to the beat. But I'll tell you, for what it's worth, that preliminary forensics has found fingerprints on the murder weapon from two separate individuals in addition to Chris."

While taking my report, Officer Edwards questioned me in some detail about Chris and my professional involvement with him, and then when we were finished he told me to contact him should Chris reach out to me in any way, urging me to save or record any text or dialogue that might transpire between "the suspect" and me.

One might assume I'd be beside myself with anguish upon leaving the police station, knowing the dire predicament Chris was presently in, but my countenance was sober and staid. I now had proof positive that he was here, and while he was wanted as a person of interest in a murder case, I could not get myself to believe he would kill someone unless driven to out of some untold manner of duplicity or self-defense. The good news was—and this might sound ironic—but the good news was that the entire SF precinct would now be looking for him, as would Officer Edwards—a man in whose core sensitivity I was beginning to trust. The prerogative I felt as a psychologist to intercept Chris was now paralleled by a police force's priority to bring him in. One thing that was crystal clear was that my patient was sinking fast, but, at the very least, his extreme behavior was making him less elusive, persuading me that he might soon be captured.

—w—

Night fell cold and hard on the mean streets of the Tenderloin, with a fog rolling in so thick that visibility was reduced to less than a block. The billowing wind blew against my clothes with an adamant indifference, but my makeshift attire was holding fast against it; indeed, my dual-layer football sweats and leather motorcycle jacked served as a shell, repelling the misty affront like the curved bow of an armored ship. I realized rather quickly that, had I not swapped my tropical rags for these Romanesque things, the unrelenting sea mist would have penetrated through the very threads. I only hoped that Chris had the gumption to pack along some warmer clothes than what I'd witnessed in the video.

Due to the limited visibility, I glided down to the more abundantly lit and peopled Market Street, from where I searched for Chris in fast food eateries, music stores, and clothing shops, and in the underground subway stations. These are the sort of places he might be drawn to commit another act of goodwill or blunt instinct offense, or so I surmised in the spurning brume.

While I was descending into the 5th Street mass transit station, a text came in from James Hopkins:

James here. Have not heard back from Chris yet. Probably ditched his Hawaii number when left. No reply from email either. Tell me if you hear from him & I'll do the same.

To which I replied, as I proceeded up the opposite escalator to ensure a signal upon sending:

Ok thanks. He may be under stress from the big move & some emotional turmoil, too. You know he's had a hard life—but don't tell him all that. If he contacts you, pls just keep him engaged, find out where he is & invite him to stay with you if possible. We can help him get on better footing.

James agreed to the plan. I didn't reveal anything about Chris's true challenges in SF, because the priority was to get him in communication with someone he could trust, and if James knew his friend was wanted on suspicion of murder or what not, the drastic change in dynamic might cause Chris to disengage further.

By now, I was growing doubtful I would find Chris on the Market Street conduit, so decided to hoof it back to Fisherman's Wharf where he might appear somewhere in the fog or so I cajoled myself into retiring to my warm quarters. At any rate, it seemed like a prudent time to return to my hotel, from where I could update my notes and ramp up my search efforts online, *after* taking a hot shower. The police department maintained an online blotter of the downtown precinct for anyone to see, which might prove a better place to look for clues, under the beclouded circumstances.

I cut down Battery Street toward Fog City Diner. Now and then, a truck, taxi cab, or standard car came pushing through the mist, while the sidewalks were mostly deserted save for some after-hours commuters and derelicts slumped down in the alcoves. But once, while peering across the street through the mist, I saw an individual sitting on a short flight of steps leading to a financial building, and he appeared to be staring back at me. From what I could discern through the maritime soup, he resembled Chris to some extent, but was wearing a trench coat and so his full stature remained rather ambiguous.

I was just about to cross the street to greet him head on, when suddenly, a patrol car came cruising slowly by, and so I proceeded instead to a nearby crosswalk to forestall a jaywalking ticket.

After crossing the street, as I was backtracking up the sidewalk to encounter my suspect, he stood and began walking in the opposite direction.

I picked up my pace, and he rounded a corner. "Chris?" I called out. "Chris, is that you?"

I hastened to the corner and peered down a narrow street buffeted by tall buildings and crisscrossed with narrow alleyways, but saw no sign of the individual in question.

I continued my search several meters further, but looking down some of the darkened alleys, I deemed it wasn't safe and so turned back. In all likelihood, as with many other individuals I'd observed on the streets of this diverse city, it was just another wayward character looking for something to do with himself, and tonight I didn't need that kind of trouble.

—m—

Later, while lying in bed, I listened to more of Chris's CD over the multiuse DVD system provided in my room. The fifth song was a slow and haunting rendition of the "Tears for Fears" song, *Mad*

Dr. Steven Meyers and Quinn Haber

World, with Chris, apparently, crooning in an after-hours, cabaret style:

> *All around me are familiar faces*
> *Worn out places, worn out faces*
> *Bright and early for their daily races*
> *Going nowhere, going nowhere*
> *Their tears are filling up their glasses*
> *No expression, no expression*
> *Hide my head I want to drown my sorrow*
> *No tomorrow, no tomorrow*
>
> *And I find it kind of funny, I find it kind of sad*
> *The dreams in which I'm dying are the best I've ever had*
> *I find it hard to tell you because I find it hard to take*
> *When people run in circles it's a very, very*
> *Mad World*
>
> *Children waiting for the day they feel good*
> *Happy birthday, happy birthday*
> *Made to feel the way that every child should*
> *Sit and listen, sit and listen*
> *Went to school and I was very nervous*
> *No one knew me, no one knew me*
> *Hello teacher tell me what's my lesson*
> *Look right through me, look right through me*
>
> *And I find it kind of funny, I find it kind of sad*
> *The dreams in which I'm dying are the best I've ever had*

I find it hard to tell you because I find it hard to take
When people run in circles it's a very, very
Mad World

The number filled me with an uncertain melancholy, and so I turned off the entertainment system and went to sleep.

—m—

September 15, 2013

Eight days have transpired since my last journal entry. I've been working intensively with the police, and now James, to tighten the noose around Chris. And I've been worried to no end about a recent revelation from Officer Edwards that some officers might shoot to kill a murder suspect who violently resists arrest. Not that I think Chris would go ballistic on a police officer, but I can easily envision a policeman going rogue on him, should he attempt to fight back. The truth is, in Chris's unknown state of mind, I have no idea how he might react if cornered.

What made me decide to update my journal today was a text message that Chris had sent James earlier this morning, with explicit instructions to forward to me. It was the first time we'd heard from him since he'd decamped from Hawaii, and although desperate in tenor, it was incredibly significant because it certified that he was still at large in SF, which was the area code from which the text was placed. The message read:

My good doctor Steven Meyers, you once told me about free-dom, but there's no freedom in this world—not for me, for I am unworthy. I was born on April Fools' Day and it's plain to see, my life is a joke. I will always have a guilty conscience, from birth to HI, and now in SF. I don't deserve to live and God justly seeks to destroy me. So now I simply do all good, all the time. From sunup to sundown I labor in the service of others. I do not partake of any pleasures, I speak always good and proper things, and I deprive myself of food and sleep. But don't worry about me: even though I am forgetful at times, I try. I apologize for all the trouble I have brought to you, to my parents, and to this world, but just forget about "Chris Fields"—he no longer exists.

The text was almost immediately followed by a call from James, who said that Chris had sent him a separate message, also saying that everything was "going fine" with the move. But James remained concerned by the overall tenor of the message, and did not realize I was a doctor.

I admitted that I was a state psychologist and Chris had been in my charge before he went absent without leave.

James replied that Chris had always struggled with low self-esteem, which he attributed to Chris's crappy relationship with his parents. He offered to come down to help me find him, but I told him it would be better if he stayed up in Santa Rosa and kept trying to persuade Chris into lodging with him there as a store employee (because I knew Chris was a sucker for helpfulness). I still didn't broach the "suspicion of murder" predicament Chris was in, because I didn't want James to repel his friend for fear of harboring a fugitive, or for Chris to run further away from that allegation, as mentioned previously. Additionally, I told James to forward a message back to Chris, imploring my onetime patient to meet me somewhere in private, just to talk. James agreed.

—ᴍ—

I transferred from my Fisherman's Wharf hotel to the Hilton San Francisco Union Square, whose environs Chris seems to be operating the most frequently. A pattern had been emerging of a suspect engaging in seemingly outrageous and sometimes technically illegal "Good Samaritan" activity, which was easily identified as the hallmark of Chris. On more than one occasion, I'd nearly been on top of him. My instincts were closing the gap—I just needed to be better situated in his roughly one kilometer of dense metropolis to gain the requisite striking distance. Officer Edwards, operating out of the neighborhood SFPD Tenderloin Station, had also logged some near misses, and had been keeping me in the loop, quite literally, with more meetings behind closed doors featuring the most recent CCTV footage of Chris's seemingly audacious campaign of benevolence, the contents of which I shall presently relay.

The new video footage was captured inside a multiplex movie theatre south of Market Street. Chris, a fortnight unshaven and looking rather skinny, is seen entering a restroom on the theater's lower level, and then the next clip is from nine hours later, when he is being chased out of the restroom by theater management, and in this latter clip he is wearing what appears to be the same uniform as the theater concessionaires. Officer Edwards told me the crime for this incident was "wrongful impersonation of a theater employee." Chris had somehow gotten a hold of an employee uniform, or a likeness thereof, and changed into while in the restroom.

"But what else did he do?" I inquired. "Surely he didn't stay in the restroom the whole time."

"He did, actually, but that's not the half of it. The whole time he was in there, he was cleaning up after the patrons. You're patient is cracked, Steven, but I feel sorry for him. You know how messy those restrooms can be?"

I shook my head gloomily. "Well, that's just Chris, officer. He does those kinds of things, but is this really considered a crime?"

"Impersonating a theater worker is, yes. For example, he could've used the guise to commit theft, sabotage, rape, to extort a patron, or whatever."

"But he didn't."

"Correct, but from an objective standpoint, he might be cast as a voyeur, which would be difficult to disprove in this case."

"I really doubt he's a pervert, officer. I think he does these things out of sense of penitence, to atone for the low self-opinion his parents have indoctrinated him with."

"The theater is still deciding if they're going to press charges, but from what I can gather, if no more evidence surfaces, and if there are no complaints from customers, they might back off—after all, he cleaned their restroom all day, which, while crazy, may serve as sufficient collateral."

The next clip had been captured at one of the piers where tourists board whale-watching boats for day excursions. Chris is seen handing out orange parkas to the passengers waiting to embark. As Officer Edwards explained it, apparently not everyone had been dressed properly for the occasion, and so Chris was there, telling them that it gets chilly on the high seas and that they would benefit from the parkas. The patrons thought he worked for the tour company, so happily took the free offer, but, as it turns out, Chris had purchased the parkas from a nearby nautical equipment store.

"So if he purchased the parkas with his own money and gave them out as gifts, how is that a crime?" I inquired. "I mean, I know it's an eccentric thing to do, but how is it illegal?"

"The complaint from the whale-watching operator was that Chris had significantly dented their own sales by giving out approximately sixty free parkas. The operator has an onboard store where they sell their own parkas, and invariably a lot of customers get cold while out at sea and end up buying the company's parkas at a high premium, which serves as further advertisement because the jackets contain the business logo and website address of the operator. They intend to sue Chris for damages, which, while understandable, is probably untenable. How do you think he afforded those sixty parkas, anyway?"

"Maybe with a credit card?" I offered. "But I'll tell you, he worked all the time in Hawaii just prior to his leaving. He may be funding these giveaways with his own savings."

"Well, at least we haven't found him to be stealing anything—yet."

"And I don't imagine he would. Chris may be a desperado, officer, but he's the most virtuous desperado you could ever meet."

"But he is misguided, doctor—and that's the problem. If we are to assume he had no part in the Tenderloin murder, which would be folly to presume from a public safety perspective, but for the sake of argument, let's just pretend he is innocent, and that he's doing these other things on some sort of personal Good Samaritan mission. Even if he means well, he is not fully aware of the ramifications of his behavior. We live in a society where this type of vigilante altruism is seen as suspect, and as we have just witnessed with the boat operator, it can adversely affect capital enterprise."

"Agreed, officer, but now tell that to the store he purchased the sixty parkas from, and they probably wouldn't mind it. But I get it—meddling with the general public, and especially as it relates to business matters, can have adverse consequences."

We moved on to yet another video captured within the past week. This one was from the retail counter area of a busy post office, where people can package and ship out their letters and parcels. Chris is seen in his now soiled aloha shirt helping customers wrap their items. Apparently he'd been doing that for over an hour before a postal worker noticed and chased him out. Moreover, he'd been giving customers the money to pay for the packaging material.

"And how is *this* one illegal?" I inquired.

"People really should be wrapping their own parcels and not taking help from a stranger. If the parcels were later found with contraband inside, such as drugs, weapons, or a bomb, it greatly complicates the matter having a second party involved, especially when the sender claims to not know who their wrapping assistant was."

"Ah, yes, I see, like at airports."

"Precisely," answered Officer Edwards, before continuing on to a fourth video. There were seven videos in all he shared during our meeting, but for the sake of brevity, this will be the last one I shall report—and it's a doozey.

Chris is seen in a busy cell phone store on Market Street. The video is dated on the afternoon of September 7, which would've been just a few days after his arrival in SF, and as such, his clothes still look cleanly pressed, as he perambulates about the store, more or less blending in with the other patrons while testing out various phones on display. But upon closer inspection, he appears to be tampering with the phones in an unusual manner.

Officer Edwards fast-tracks the video forward, as we observe a sped-up Chris tampering with five or six phones in total, before a store employee approaches him. They exchange some brief dialogue and then Chris causally exits the store.

A follow-up video was captured at 1:50 p.m. the next day, when a delivery person is seen entering the store with a large box, which he drops off at the front counter. An employee, who we might assume it the manager, opens the box, reads a letter inside, and then starts removing the contents, appearing entirely perplexed by what is transpiring.

Several minutes later, closer to 2:00 p.m., a modest rush of patrons begins queuing up behind the counter, at which point the manager distributes the contents of the box, which, when unwrapped, appear to be framed 8 × 10 photographs of the customers.

"I don't understand," I put to Officer Edwards.

"Neither would I," he conceded, "unless I read the complaint. In the first video I showed you from the previous day, Chris was clandestinely returning data memory cards back into the display phones."

"Returning them?"

"The complainant alleges that earlier that same day, Chris was in the store testing out the display phones, particularly the camera feature, taking photographs of himself and other customers, and helping them to take selfies. The complainant alleges they have no CCTV footage of that incident, because the machine was undergoing a reboot and had not yet been reactivated by the store employees, but they allege that Chris was also handing out money."

I shrugged my shoulders, entirely nonplussed.

"And so," the officer continued with a hint of relish, "Chris had been capturing photographs of people, and then telling them to return to the store at 2:00 p.m. sharp the next day to received a free framed picture of themselves. He went so far as to give them ten dollars apiece to add credence to his "promotional offer," which he told his beneficiaries was being promoted by the cell phone companies, separate from the store."

"A peculiar mind that boy has," I offered, "but very much to his benevolent nature. So he was using the store's display phones to help people take selfies, and then he gave them a cash gift, along with their framed pictures to pick up the next day, all beneath the store's radar."

"Got it—right under their noses. The crime was in his removing the data cards from the store, from where he took them to a nearby photo studio to have the pictures developed and framed, and then he paid the studio to deliver the pictures back to the store at 1:45 p.m. the next day, along with a letter he wrote to the store manager explaining that customers would shortly be arriving to claim their free framed photos."

I knew Chris well enough, but still, the complexity of his shenanigan, and the fact that he pulled it off, caused me to go, "*Pfft!*"

"So you can see, Doctor, your patient believes he's doing good here, but in fact he is causing a lot of problems in my precinct, and he's unlikely to stop until we catch him or, god forbid, until he pisses off the wrong person."

"I know, I know," I lamented, shaking my head. "It's too bad—but we will find him."

"For his sake, I hope we do, and soon."

September 22, 2013

It is Sunday. Another week has lapsed in my mainland escapade, and I emphasize "mainland" because my job situation back in "the islands" has reared its stern aloft like a sinking ship preparing for its final plunge to a watery grave.

Earlier this week, Sue had been shooting me with emails, warning she could only keep up the leave without pay "guise" for so long until she would be "forced" to generate a Termination from State Service Form and report my "true activities" there, and then she would "necessitate" the signatures of her superiors in order to "actuate" my "permanent dismissal"—i.e., she was telling me in a poorly polite, office-politics way that she intended to have me fired.

And so, two days ago, on Friday morning, I emailed her with a final, urgent request to wait "just a few more workdays."

She has not since responded, and so tonight I feel rather desperate. Her ultimatum has compelled me to stay on Chris's case 24/7. I wish to end this charade and not lose my job, but yet I am practically seeing his reflection in the downtown windows, and so damn me if I capitulate to defeat at this late stage of the game.

September 24, 2103
A cold and violent windstorm struck downtown SF this evening, with terrific gusts concentrating between the buildings and knocking out multiple power lines, traffic lights, and signage affixed to lampposts, etc., while dead leaves, trash, and street gunk has been strewn everywhere. Even though Chris has not been seen in more than a week, if he is still out there, tonight I feel sorry for him. I've been drinking more each day, and late into the evenings.

September 26, 2013
All signs of Chris have gone cold, and so to save my job, tomorrow I shall throw in the towel and let the police handle it.

September 27, 2103
This morning, as I was browsing online for a plane ticket home, James called, and then texted me a link to a three-minute YouTube video that had recently gone viral. I first viewed it on my cell phone, and then on my laptop to make certain we weren't deceiving ourselves.

It was Chris Fields, standing in broad daylight upon a flagpole dais at the entrance of Pier 39, the main shopping pier in Fisherman's Wharf, and most significantly, it was time-stamped and posted on September 24, just under three days ago. As far as

James was concerned, if Chris wasn't pulling one over on everyone, he demonstrably was in a bad way and needed professional help ASAP.

In the video, entitled, "Homeless man takes blame for JFK plot," and tagged to SF, Chris looks like a longtime, flagellant street person, with messy, matted hair forming into knotted clumps, an unkempt beard stretching down his neck, sallow and dirty, sucked in cheeks with a safety pin poked through one side and drawing blood from his hirsute face—a brutal and cheap gimcrack from which a small chain drapes down from his black painted lips and connects to a bloodstained, paperclip earring. His objectionable visage is complemented by a matted and torn, black trench coat, beneath which his badly soiled aloha shirt is broken open at the buttons, revealing a bony, emaciated chest; his khakis, too, are direly rent, nigh exposing his genitals, while his shoes and socks are split open at the front like a loosely packed bologna sandwich, revealing dirty, swollen, black and purple toes. He is standing there, in this flagrantly degenerate state, beneath a storm-ragged Old Glory and frayed Pier 39 banner, where, with unsteady balance like a drunkard prone to falling over, he has garnered the attention of a small crowd of onlookers as he proclaims with delayed histrionics, gesticulating awkwardly while shaking almost spasmodically:

"I'm here to tell you that I'm sorry when you see me coming, and so you cross the street because you're afraid of me. I would rather give you money or clean your house than have you think about me like that. I am guilty of a great many things, but will try harder to be of service to you. I have played party to theft arrests, I have seen hundreds of thousands of trees chopped down just beyond the forest lines of the freeways, where passers-by can't see it, and I've seen mountains of pollution dumped into the sea, and all of these things I take responsibility for. I am guilty. I do not say 'save the planet,' and I don't know whether to choose paper or plastic."

The crowd sniggers in uncomfortable amusement at what appears to the ranting of a man unhinged.

"From every small thing," he continues his diatribe of self-incrimination, "from every little time I bother you when I'm crossing the street too slowly as you seek to turn right or left, to ever bigger things, such as the incrimination of Bernie Madoff and Enron, I am the chief troublemaker in all these things."

Now there is general laughter in the crowd, with one onlooker shouting, "Can you prove it?"

"You know not what I do," Chris rejoins, "and that's the problem: I am a sinner too much in private, and so I am here today to proclaim to you in public that I have a million and two skeletons in my closet: I am a thief and a murderer, responsible for the assassination of JFK."

"How'd you do it?!" a man shouts out, perhaps humoring him on, while someone else cries for pier security.

"I took it upon myself to make Lee Harvey Oswald do it," Chris replies.

"When were you born, anyway?" the banterer continues.

Chris rubs his forehead and says, "I can't remember."

The crowd erupts into guffaws.

"No, no, please—you must believe me! I have a way of doing these things!" Chris implores. "You know Grimace, of McDonalds and the McDonald land commercials? Rest assured that it is because of I, that he was taken away."

A renewed brouhaha emanates from the throng, inducing Chris to shout above them while gesticulating wildly: "You *must* believe me, ladies and gentlemen! At the Golden Arches, new lines opened up and it bothered those whose shoulders I tapped, and suddenly the big purple touchy-feely guy was gone! Grimace was the fall guy for my transgressions, and Aunt Jemima will be next!"

Chris goes off balance and grabs the flagpole to keep from falling over, while some of the spectators standing toward the front had seen enough and begin to filter off.

My onetime star patient, now appearing no more than a shameful, mad, raving drunk, stables himself enough to reach into his trench coat, where he appears to fumble at pulling something cumbersome out.

The crowd emits a collective shriek of terror and cowers back, believing he is about to whip out a rifle and commit mass murder, when suddenly, fistfuls of quarters and individually wrapped Ghirardelli chocolates come soaring out of his hands.

The panic-stricken spectators are now seen tumbling over one another in an unbridled contest to scoop up the bounty, which Chris continues to liberally dispense until he sees pier security pulling up beside the rabble on a golf cart.

Just before the video ends, Chris hobbles off on the opposite side of the crowd of the private security officers, who cannot so easily traverse or get around the ruckus. He appears to escape onto the main drag, which is connected by many more piers and potential hiding places, and so for all intents and purposes, Chris flew the coop with impunity, leaving naught but a trail of candy, quarters, and a viral video in his absence.

I forwarded the YouTube link to Officer Edwards with a note that Chris was recently active in the area, and looks much different now. His trench coat, black lipstick, and pierced cheek, I specified, should make him much easier to find.

Officer Edwards was quick to thank me, saying it was a good lead that he had no prior knowledge of.

How Chris has evaded us all week was anyone's guess, but he appeared to have undergone a makeover for the worse, while his physical condition was flagging to the extreme. In seeing him so wantonly undernourished and mocked by a public nescient to his internal tribulations, I committed myself to staying until the end of the month. I texted Sue with an ultimatum, because I knew that's how she preferred to resolve things, promising that if I wasn't back by next week, I would knowingly forfeit my position with the State of Hawaii. I told her that I was very close to catching Chris, who was recently seen in desperate straits.

She replied with a simple thumbs-up, which meant I was barely holding on.

I returned my focus to the waterfront area where I'd originally lodged, and now knew the topography well enough to sweep the nooks where Chris might be hiding out, while he planned his next audacious act.

September 28, 2103

I've been working closely with the police, and our dragnet has yielded a few near captures—but Chris has only been showing himself at night, and we've always been just minutes too late. We suspect he may periodically decamp to the dense foliage around

Coit Tower, or to the Chestnut and Kearny open space area, or even to the Presidio of San Francisco Park—if he could traverse that far in his reportedly famished condition. Any day now, any hour—any minute, his trial of self-renunciation might be over.

A message from Chris to James tonight hinted at the former's present state. Chris texted him the lyrics to a song entitled, *Born to Die in the Gutter*, from a band they both like called, Discharge. The lyrics read:

> *Homeless and alone, hungry and cold*
> *Born to die, to die in the gutter*
> *Dying of exposure in the cold night*
> *Homeless and alone, hungry and cold*
> *Left for death in the cold night*

James added that, normally he wouldn't be concerned about their swapping of song lyrics because that was something they did before. But under the present circumstances, he took the message as a thinly veiled mayday that Chris's straits were mortally dire. The overnight temperature had been cooling significantly recently, and so I didn't doubt there was a chilling reality behind the message.

September 30, 2103
It was a cold and foggy morning near the Embarcadero waterfront. Police sirens blared in the distance. The United States was in the midst of a major budget crisis as House leaders sparred over President Obama's Affordable Care Act, and for the first time in seventeen years, the US Government was on the verge of shutting

down. But here, on Monday morning in the SF Financial District, the flurry of rush hour commuters signaled business as usual for this city in clover.

I'd been on the hunt for Chris since dawn, with early morning police chatter and messages from James helping me to triangulate his position near the E*Trade building on Sansome Street—or so my instincts were conferring. Officer Edwards, on duty at the Tenderloin Precinct, had messaged me that a black trench coated "drifter" had been seen loitering near the top of the steps of the Stock Exchange Building, bringing concern to some of the premarket brokers.

I was now one-half block away from the Stock Exchange, making haste toward the intersection of Bush and Sansome streets, when before me beyond the crosswalk I spotted a drove of oncoming businesspeople maneuvering over and around a heap of trash on the sidewalk. I at first ignored the higgledy-piggledy spectacle of urbanity, and was about to turn left on Bush Street, when suddenly, I glimpsed what appeared to be a hand momentarily rise up from the rubbish. A businessman clutching a briefcase stopped and seemed to castigate the clump of refuse, but it was difficult for me to clearly ascertain his histrionics through the approaching foot traffic. As the horde came rushing into the crosswalk in an attempt to beat the flashing "Don't Walk" sign, the interloper in question followed fast on their heels.

I tried to stop and ask this passerby, as the "Don't Walk" signal turned a solid red, prohibiting my own crossing, what he'd seen over there that caused him to stop and cast aspersions down upon, to which he replied, barely breaking stride and forcing me to hasten alongside: "Just another bum blocking the way, you know, *'Give me, give me, give me!'* I told him to get out of the goddamn way and stop asking us working stiffs for handouts to buy more booze with."

With the scream of patrol sirens sweeping closer, I dodged through vehicle traffic in the interdicted crosswalk and then jostled through pedestrians amassed on the opposite sidewalk as I endeavored toward the derelict in question, at last coming upon the most distressing moment in my entire life.

Chris Fields lay there, heaped up and withering away beneath his black trench coat. He was emaciated, long unshaven, wounded in one eye, and barely recognizable save for his now thoroughly demolished aloha shirt and khaki slacks. His cruel facial embellishments were also in gory evidence, matching the harrowing bijouterie captured in the viral video several days antecedent, only now, his lacerations were direly infected.

"Please give me, pl—please give me . . ." the poor braddah repeated deliriously, lifting his skeletal hand while opening a dirty palm, apparently not even recognizing me.

I grasped his hand between mine. It was bony and cold to the touch. I tried to rub it warm, imploring, "Chris it's me, Doctor Meyers! My lord! What has happened to you?"

But my words seemed to have little effect on my half-blind friend, who continued his solicitation, stammering as if in rote, "pl—please give me, the chance to help you."

Businesspeople continued to trample all around us, one harried seigneur tripping over and lambasting, "Get out of the middle of the sidewalk, dumbasses!"

And then Chris latched onto my shirt and looked beyond me, toward the sky. His blackened lips eased into a smile, and then his body fell, seemingly weightless, into my arms.

I cried out *help!*—*ambulance!*—as Chris remained with his head and arms falling back in my embrace.

A swarm of policemen descended upon us then, with Officer Edwards leading the charge. My patient wasn't breathing and had no pulse. An ambulance arrived shortly thereafter, and he was conveyed inside and swept away.

Officer Edwards took me in the back of his patrol car and we raced with all sirens blaring to the district hospital, where Chris was pronounced DOA.

I lunged upon my patient's vacant body, weeping with sovereign anguish: "I'm so, so, sorry, Chris. I'm sorry that I wasn't in time."

October 1, 2013
"Yesterday, Chris Fields died in my arms," I relayed with trembling voice. "He'd been homeless in SF, and appeared to have succumbed to the elements. I shall be coming home once I figure out his burial situation. His parents might not care, but we, as human beings, owe him a decent burial."

Sue was crestfallen, saying, "I'm so sorry to hear that, especially after what you put yourself through."

"What about my termination? Is that still active?"

"You're still on leave without pay, but when you get back, we'll need talk about what happens next. But I'll tell you now: I won't allow myself to be compromised by your transgression, not now, or ever again."

"Okay, well thank you for your understanding, I guess."

I did not regret my actions, but neither did I wish to lose my job, if that wasn't already a foregone conclusion. A fortnight at the

Hilton Union Square on leave without pay had delivered a double whammy to me financially, and while I was still doing okay on savings, I did not wish to take further losses if I could help it. But there was one more loose end money-wise that, for the sake of Chris's good conduct, needed to be addressed. He had paid his rent for September, and now, on October first, he was deceased. I phoned his landlord and informed him that I would be paying Chris's rent for October, as his last month's rent.

The slumlord was recalcitrant and waged a protest, claiming. "Chris already sent rent for October, but is on a one-year lease that doesn't renew until March. He cannot break the lease now, or I can sue for the remaining balance. I have my own bills to pay."

"Sir, yesterday, Chris Fields perished. I was there."

"Oh really? And can you prove it?"

"Yes."

There was a pause on the line, and then a ruffling as if in rumination or frustration, after which he rejoined: "I want to see the death paper then, and for your sake, you better not be playing me or I'll come at you for accessory to blackmail."

"I assure you, sir, such is not the case."

I then arranged, not without further resistance, to come by the apartment within a week to deliver Chris's last rent check and to remove his belongings, which I planned to store at my rental unit until a final decision was made from any and all concerned parties on what to do with them. Thankfully, the parsimonious landlord would not be there to assist me, but instructed me to leave the rent check in an envelope with his name on it in the foyer drawer.

October 2, 2013
Today, Officer Edwards shared Chris's coronary report with me, which indicated he died of "cardiac arrhythmia brought on by severe electrolyte imbalance," i.e., starvation. It was further noted that his left temporal lobe was swollen with a mild hemorrhage. This is the part of the brain responsible for hearing, language, and memory. The concussion may have caused Chris to lapse in and out of amnesia while in SF.

October 3, 2013
Officer Edwards called me back into his office, saying he had, "Two significant items pertaining to the wrap of Chris Fields' case," that I might be interested in.

The first exhibit was a rearview dash-cam clip of the murder that Chris had apologized for, thereby essentially implicating himself in. The video was mailed in anonymously by someone who'd captured it on his or her vehicle's rear camera while idling at a traffic signal. There is an altercation between two men on the sidewalk not far behind and adjacent to the vehicle, which ends in their stabbing each other. As the vehicle filming the incident begins to advance away from the scene, one of the wounded suspects—suspect #1—is seen rounding the corner toward the Nob Hill hotel, while the other—suspect #2—turns and plows directly into Chris, who'd just emerged from a blind alley. As suspect #2 falls to the ground bleeding, Chris somehow ends up holding his murder weapon. Chris stays with him momentarily, but then appears to hear something and so continues around the next corner where suspect #1 had fled. The footage is then blocked by parked cars, as the vehicle filming the scene pulls further ahead.

Officer Edwards explained, "From here, we know from the preexisting footage that suspect #1 drops dead in front of the hotel as Chris emerges behind him holding the murder weapon. But we now have this prequel clearly showing what actually transpired. Just as I'd originally assumed, it was a drug deal gone bad, with Chris having no direct involvement: he was merely in the wrong place at the wrong time and got caught up in the finale of the fatal melee, when suspect #2 handed him his murder weapon perhaps intentionally, or perhaps by happenstance."

I nervously rubbed my beard in contemplation of the incident, which had been disturbing to watch.

"And so," Officer Edwards concluded, "for what it's worth, Chris has posthumously been absolved of suspicion of murder."

"It's worth a lot, actually," I replied.

"And then there's this," he continued, handing me a small manila envelope. "It's Chris's death video on an SD card. You can watch it at home if you want, but I don't care to relive this kind of stuff if I can help it."

"Jesus. Was someone filing on their cell phone or something?"

"It was captured from an overhead traffic signal cam—you know, the kind we use to issue citations by mail. This is your copy, but we've already reviewed it and there's nothing more to see. You arrived on the scene seconds before us, and Chris died of natural causes."

"Malnutrition."

"A heart attack, doctor, but you know what I mean. I can't stand these instances of self-infliction, the slow suicide of people who give up, as society gives up on them."

"I understand, Tom—it's the bane of our time, and disturbs me to no end. But I think Chris was a different type of person: he never gave up on society, as society gave up on itself."

He regarded me with raised brows, as if he found my statement something of a curiosity. He rubbed the sleepy-seeds from the corners of his eyes, and then eased. "Well, that's it then, doc. If anything else comes up, you know where to reach me."

"Thank-you, sir," I offered, and we resolutely shook hands.

"No, thank-you, Steven, thanks for coming out. I'm only sorry it had to end like this."

"Nope, I'm all good, man," I said, my voice beginning to crack. I thumped my fist twice against my heart to check myself, but it was no use . . . I broke down weeping.

Tom embraced me and patted my back emphatically.

It wasn't until I'd made a flight reservation, departing for Honolulu the next morning, organized my sparse belongings, eaten a heavy meal and taken a long shower; it wasn't until I'd fixed myself a rum and coke, and another, that I was able to power up my laptop and watch the death video. I'd needed some sort of procession, a lustration to do it—the finalization that I was irrevocably leaving SF, before I could face the painful denouement once again. But it had to be done. Something deep inside me hankered after the closure that only an objective perspective might bring, no matter how distressing.

The footage was captured from an overhead traffic post, looking down on the scene at an approximately forty-five degree angle. It begins with me rushing up to Chris, and then, as pedestrians practically trample us, he dies in my arms, I call out for help, and the police descend upon us. That's it—a twenty-two second clip.

But there is something peculiar about it, barely noticeable, that I just can't place. So I run the video again.

The drama, filmed in color, unfolds while the traffic light is changing from green, to yellow, to red. But the light fixture itself seems to be slightly skewed, as if perhaps it'd been damaged by the recent windstorm, for it casts a subtle, coruscated cone or ring ray effect across the surface of the lens as the signal changes colors. In addition, the sunlight overhead breaks through the fog just as Chris is dying, further affecting the image with a faint but ever-increasing light flare effect.

I alter the image with aftereffects such as exposure, balance, sharpen, and contrast, then run it again. There *is* something more going on in the video, like a second layer hiding somewhere within the settings. I set the clip on loop and keep tweaking it.

There's something in the fog, a wraith-like figure which becomes more distinct as I work it out. It descends upon us when the light is green, to when Chris falls listless in my arms, and then rises again as the sun gains strength and the traffic light changes to yellow, and then disappears overhead when the light turns red and the police close in.

I take another rum, straight, and then continue editing, my hands beginning to sweat and my eyes opening wide as I trap the thing further into shape. The nebulous image, a fog-borne wraith, descends as a misty, pulsating blotch, and then when it is upon Chris and I, it takes a more certain form as a hominid-shaped specter, and finally when it rises again, it appears to have wings. I spit out my rum. The angelic presence passes before the camera conveying a ghostly revenant of Chris in its bosom, its wings gently flapping as it takes flight, and then, as the traffic light turns yellow, there is a radiant, carousel lens flare, into which the angel holding Chris disappears in a flash of light. The signal turns red and I am left on the sidewalk, holding the shell of Chris and calling out for help as the police close in.

Nodding in tears, I hit save, and then watch the copy about twenty more times, at last ejecting the small plastic card and placing it, with trembling hands, back into the envelope, whereupon I shakily pen, "Chris Fields" death footage, case closed.

I know what I saw, and believe it is real—that's not the issue. What I don't intend to do is trivialize Chris's passing into the form of an urban legend. I reread my scrawl, and then toss the envelope back onto the desk, where it lands, paper-light as if there's nothing at all inside.

October 5, 2013

Yesterday I repaired to Hawaii, and today I returned to Chris's apartment to drop off his "last month's rent" and itemize his belongings. While thumbing through some sheet music he'd left on his piano, I came upon a number entitled, *My Mind's Diseased*, composed by a band called Battalion of Saints. Chris had penciled in additional accents, codas, rests, and other musical notations, apparently adapting the piece to his own plaintive style. In fact, the whole composition appeared to be transposed an octave down. The lyrics, which he left unaltered, pained me to read:

> *Day and night I look around and see*
> *My whole life is caving in on me*
> *My mind's diseased with daily life*

Some days I wish I'd hurry up and die
To relieve the pressure that's inside my head

All these problems, there's no escape
From all these pressures in my mind
These endless days and sleepless nights
I sometimes wonder what keeps me alive
The thoughts keep pounding in my brain
There's only one way to alleviate this pain

I set the music down upon the keys and lowered my head in a paroxysm of grief.

When I gained the gumption to look up again, I discovered a note on the music rack. It was Chris's last will and testament, or his version thereof, written in cursive.

It stated only:

Upon my death, please give my piano and all my belonging to charity.
Chris Fields, September 3, 2013

Had I only discovered this on the night of his fleeing, I would've had sufficient cause to request his detainment at SFO, perhaps under the precept of a parole violation. But now that he was gone, that was immaterial, as was his hallowed soul.

There was a short stack of books on the floor nearby. I turned my attention to the text on top, entitled, *The Imitation of Christ*. Its back cover blurb denoted it "an acclaimed religious treatise," penned by an early fifteenth-century German monk named Thomas à Kempis. Remarkably, it was thought to be, "a devotional classic second in popularity only to the Bible."

There was a bookmark within, leading to some highlighted passages, and these last articles of Chris that I read would prove sufficient enough to enlighten me to perhaps his most pragmatic philosophic influence. And so I will end this journal with the words he selected from the text of Thomas à Kempis:

Do not be pleased with yourself about your ability or talent, lest you displease God, from whom comes the sum of whatever natural good you have. Do not think you are better than others, lest you appear worse in God's eyes; God knows what we are. Do not be proud of your good deeds, for God's judgments differ from ours, and he is often displeased by what pleases us.

If you have any good qualities, believe that other people have better ones; by doing so you will retain your humility. It does you no harm if you place yourself beneath everyone else; it does you great harm, though, if you place yourself above even one other person. A person who is humble is always at peace, but a proud person carries a heart filled with envy and resentment.

—

Conclusion

My name is Quinn Haber. I am Dr. Meyers' editorial assistant on this project. He decided to publish his journal as a way for him to find his own closure on the case, being a "thorough, obsessive man of letters, regiment, and completion," as he termed it. He has here accorded me the opportunity to include some additional details concerning his account, which we believe will better encapsulate it into a complete narrative for formal release. This should not be construed as an attempt to embroider it with colorful dramatizations, but is merely a duty we felt to better satisfy Chris's story.

At the lawful dictate of his father, Chris's body was cremated in SF, and the cremation authority was instructed to *dispose of* the cremated remains. This should be no surprise coming from Gerald Fields, as it was the cheapest possible option. A one-line death notice, posted in a secondary SF newspaper, was included in the bargain-basement offer. It read: "Chris Fields, April 1, 1989–September 30, 2013." There was no death notice or obituary published in Chris's hometown of Florence, South Carolina, nor in Honolulu, Hawaii, where he had labored so diligently to raise himself out of debt while placating others.

As for Chris's death video, Dr. Meyers shared it with me in person several times over the course of our corroboration. Using his laptop, he would show me the raw footage, and then enhance it in real-time for me to observe his methodology, employing nothing beyond the after-effects capabilities of any standard contemporary photography interface app or software, i.e., he was not engaging the likes of Photoshop or anything so fundamentally transformative. Yet, the imagery produced by his basic enhancements was so convincing that I agreed *not* to make it public because it would certainly go viral, and he wished not to sensationalize Chris's story, and especially Chris's death, with a pop culture "paranormal" video.

Dr. Meyers' other concern was that too much public attention to the footage could draw the spotlight onto his employer in Hawaii. Pointed questions might be asked about why a Hawaii state psychologist, ostensibly working on Hawaii state time, was with his patient in California at the time of his patient's death: hot-button political questions of the type his executive director was working hard to preclude. This was an era of government shutdowns and fiscal hawkishness, lending credence to her paranoia. Dr. Meyers had narrowly lost his job before he and Sue settled on covering up, in perpetuity, his part in the SF episode, while Karen B., the care coordinator, also gave her vow of silence because she didn't want to see a scandal result from Dr. Meyer's "act of love," as she contextualized it. Thus, the actual names of individuals and their employers have been altered in this book to maintain confidentiality, with the Disclaimer to follow further obfuscating the attested players.

Finally, in regard to a decisive medical diagnosis or psycho-analytical conclusion for "Chris's case," in the end, Dr. Meyers chose not to provide any. The young man was now deceased, he lamented, and so it no longer seemed important or relevant to attempt to categorize the totality of the individual that Chris was with an ICD-9 code or a truncated textbook definition. We decided that this book—the faithful journal in which Dr. Meyers kept about him—would be as far as we would attempt to bind Chris to a world that he never felt he belonged to. And while Chris denied any claim to religiosity, Dr. Meyers concluded that, if asked about his patient, he could only report with any certainty that Chris was a good Christian.

Disclaimer

This is a psychological drama. All characters and dialogue, and all incidents, with the exception of some well-known historical and public incidents, are products of the authors' imaginations and are not to be construed as real. Any semblance to similar characters or events extraneous to this work is entirely coincidental and purely unintentional by the authors.

Other Great Titles from Phantasea Books

(Listed in alphabetical order)

Echoes from the Sun: A Modern Quest for the Fountain of Youth, by Ari Marsh

The Heart of a Traveler: Reflections from the Fathomless Edge of the World, by Ari Marsh

I Fell in Love with an Aleutian Vampire: The WWII in Adak Commemorative Edition, by Jake Harper and Quinn Haber

Islands on the Fringe: A Year of Micronesian Waves and Wanderers, by S. Jacques Stratton

Old Lanai (Illustrated): A True Ghost Story from Hawaii, by Warren S. Croft

The Somali Pirate, by Noor Fayrus and Quinn Haber

The Somali Pirate 2: Dagger Dogs of Zayid, by Noor Fayrus and Quinn Haber

The Somali Pirate 3: White Star Empire, by Noor Fayrus and Quinn Haber

Tonkin, by Quinn Haber

The Volcano Trilogy: A Philippines Surfing Odyssey, by Quinn Haber

Dr. Steven Meyers and Quinn Haber

PhantaSea Books